I0581846

The Forbidden Island

Published by:
Powder River Publishing LLC
1014 Black Mountain Road
Thermopolis, Wyoming 82443

Copyright © 2025
ISBN: 978-1-956881-57-8
Printed in the United States of America

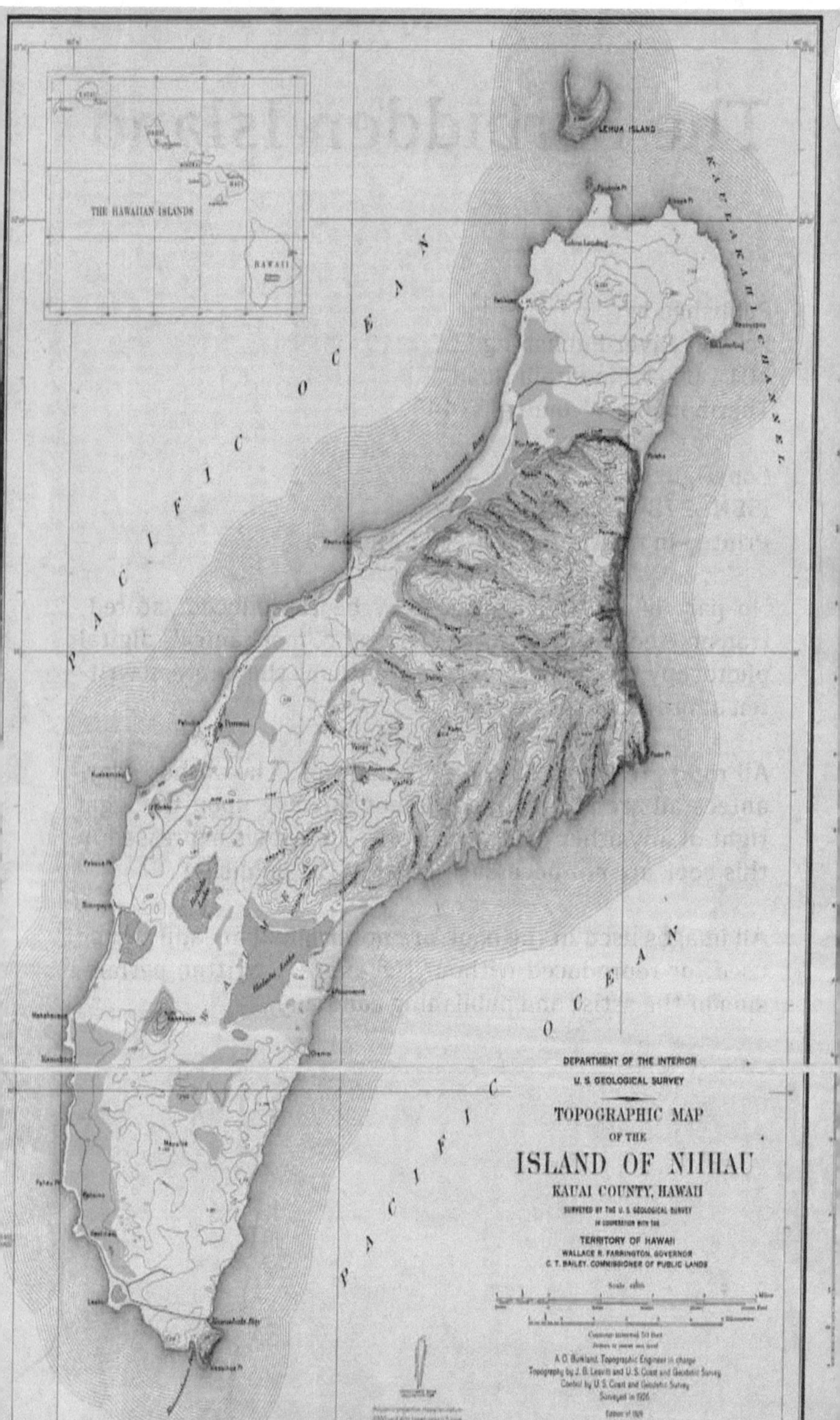

THE HAWAIIAN ISLANDS
LEHUA ISLAND
KAULAKAHI CHANNEL
PACIFIC OCEAN
DEPARTMENT OF THE INTERIOR
U. S. GEOLOGICAL SURVEY
TOPOGRAPHIC MAP
OF THE
ISLAND OF NIIHAU
KAUAI COUNTY, HAWAII
SURVEYED BY THE U. S. GEOLOGICAL SURVEY
IN COOPERATION WITH THE
TERRITORY OF HAWAII
WALLACE R. FARRINGTON, GOVERNOR
C. T. BAILEY, COMMISSIONER OF PUBLIC LANDS
Scale
Contour interval 50 feet
Datum is mean sea level
A. O. Burkland, Topographic Engineer in charge
Topography by J. B. Leavitt and U. S. Coast and Geodetic Survey
Control by U. S. Coast and Geodetic Survey
Surveyed in 1926
Edition of 1929

Dedication

To my son and daughter, who are my sun and moon. I love you with all my heart and soul.

The Haole

The morning sun burned through faint wispy clouds, misting cooly on the points of Niʻihau island.

Monk Seals bathed freely on the stretched white sand beaches, startled by the sound of an approaching plane and its struggling propeller.

"The fuel tank took a bullet," the Japanese fighter pilot, Shigenori Nishikaichi, thought to himself. He looked behind his fighter plane at the leaking fuel.

The lifeblood of his craft bled out slowly. "There's no way I'll make it back to the carrier Hiryu."

The 22-year-old first-class airmen descended to the island of Niʻihau they said was uninhabited before the attack. It was the designated crash landing spot for the Hawaiʻi Operation. He was briefed on what to do in this kind of situation. There would be a submarine coming to rescue any stranded airmen.

Rescue would await him here on this small island. All he had to do was survive the landing and wait it out until help arrived.

"There will be a submarine after me and I will join the victory celebration on the carrier Hiryu," he told himself, creating the optimism he knew would be needed to make it out of this situation alive. "And what a glorious victory it was today."

He thought of his father and his mother back home in Hashihama, Japan. He thought of all the choices leading him to this moment. He could remember the day he became an airman and the feeling it brought to his soul. It was a feeling of destiny at the time and he felt it ever-present now. This was a part of that destiny and he would make it back to his family, he told himself. That's what he was going to do.

The Northern end of Niʻihau island is a long stretch of beach, culminating in the nearby cliffs, leading up to the extinct volcano crater. Shigenori witnessed goats jumping on the cliffside as he dropped rapidly in elevation to the sound of the failing machine beginning to lose power.

"It's not going to hold out much longer." Shige scanned the island below for a proper place to set the plane down without losing his life in the process.

The plane drifted around a bend when the sight of a white building flooded into view. People dressed in Sunday whites were going into the building with some looking up at the plane with surprised faces.

Shige was shocked when he spotted people on the island he had been told was deserted and uninhabited.

"What else don't I know about this island?" Shige thought to himself, his mind now drowning in fear that was flooding in by the second.

If only he could make another pass around the island to think it over and find a more suitable landing location away from residents, he thought.

There had been a mistake in believing the island was not inhabited. One of the few mistakes made that day by the Japanese.

Shige eyed the land below for a suitable spot to lay the Zero down that had taken him this far through the battle he had participated in. He and his countrymen had brought utter destruction to the American fleet that morning in the attack. Shige's plane was one of a handful of Japanese planes damaged that morning.

Shige spotted a perfect landing spot below in what appeared to be a natural runway in the form of a dry lake.

Nearly six years prior, the Navy reported to the United States Department of Defense that the Japanese would one day use the island of Niʻihau as an invasion point to launch an air offensive against Pearl Harbor and the island of Oahu. The Navy and advanced scouts believed the dry lakes on the island of Niʻihau would make a suitable runway for the Japanese Air Force.

The Robinson family has privately owned the island of Niʻihau since 1864 and took the report very seriously at the time. In response to this information, the Robinson family and most notably Alymer Robinson and his foreman, dug 14,000 miles of 18-inch trench in the sandy dry lakes. They used rocks to break up areas that were not plowed to make those impassable as well. These very lakes the Navy envisioned would be used as a future airport to house such an invasion force by the Japanese were spotted by Shige as he came barreling down from above.

The 22-year-old pilot was just 16 when the American Navy gave a stark prediction of future relations between the United States and Japan. The Navy believed a war would intersect between the two superpowers on the island of Ni'ihau. On December 7, 1941, part of that prediction became a reality.

Shige killed his throttle, quieting the engine.

He held his breath.

The nose of the aircraft, pointing towards the dry lake, became like a lead sinker for Shige to control. The aircraft grew closer to the ground and he could see the trench, knowing that it was going to destroy his landing gear on impact and possibly end his life. It was too late to change anything and he hoped for the best, gritting his teeth in anticipation of what was to come.

He was willing to die that day. That did not bother him as much as not meeting his comrades on the carrier Hiryu after the successful mission he had prepared for so meticulously with his brothers in arms for months now. The thought of his family crept into the back of his mind for a moment, and he reassured himself that he would one day see them again and this was just another bump on the road to glory.

As the ground came nearer and nearer, seconds became millennia as time became incandescent and absolute. He felt everything in that moment.

The wheels touched down, followed by a thunderous explosion of sound. The chaos vibrated every corner of the island announcing itself in reverberations of dirt and steel mixing with rock.

The landing gear violently dislodged from lava rock laden just below the surface, throwing the pilot into convulsions of unpredictable movement as the plane scrambled to a halt on a barbed wire fence.

The rocks had been lying in that field from the time the shield volcano responsible for creating Ni'ihau last exploded underwater around three and a half million years ago, leaving them as mementos of the fiery past to be dragged back and forth by the sea, and then eventually man.

The plane didn't go far after touching down on the island and meeting the trench, smashing the pilot's head against the controls when the plane finally stopped on the fence.

Shigenori was delirious as he tried to reach

for his gun and simultaneously tried to collect the important battle plans he had onboard.

Startled by the plane crashing in the field, 29-year-old Harold Kaleohano watched the scene unfold before his frozen eyes less than 100 yards away from his front porch. He was picking ti leaves outside his house for chicken lau lau later that evening when he heard the sound of the plane coming down to earth. He turned just in time to catch the entire event as he ran as fast as he could to the scene of the crash.

Kaleohano was born on the Big Island of Hawai'i and spoke English perfectly, and Hawaiian.

"The others will have surely heard the trouble and will come running," Harold thought to himself. He had never seen anything like this happen before and the excitement made his stomach uneasy. The adrenaline rushed through his body as he came before the wreck, searching for survivors.

Howard ran to the cockpit of the fighter plane where he could see the pilot struggling and seemingly looking for something.

Howard, knowing there had been a recent oil embargo placed on the Japanese by the Americans, recognized the markings on the plane as foreign and Japanese.

"It's a Japanese plane," Howard said to himself. "They must be in the area looking to make trouble for Oahu, or Kaua`i."

He looked at the man in the plane and thought him dead. On second glance, Howard saw the pilot was still breathing. He knew the pilot would die if he did not act and get the man out of the plane.

The pilot stopped moving as Howard put his hands on the cockpit. There was silence. Then the pilot moved in sudden violent contortions of frantic breath, startling Howard as he tried to find a way to open the cockpit.

Howard could see a pistol waiting on the pilot's holster. He strained to open the hatch and after a few tries, succeeded in his task and opened the plane to the outside world.

The pilot did not move much, half in and out of consciousness when the cockpit was flung open. Howard took the opportunity to collect the pilot's pistol. He gently removed it from the holster with the utmost care and caution.

Howard looked at the pistol for a minute before carefully stashing it away in his hip like he had seen paniolos do.

He began looking for the pilot's identifying papers.

Quickly, he located them and began stuffing them in his pocket.

Having disarmed the pilot and possessing his identifying papers, Howard went about trying to free the pilot from the wreckage.

This proved difficult as the Hawaiian

heaved and hoed with all his might to free the pilot from his confines amongst the doomed plane. Howard was about the same size as the pilot as he used all his might to free the man from his would be tomb.

The plane sent out billowing waves of smoke increasing with intensity and volume as every second passed, making it hard to breathe.

The gasoline had all but emptied out of the fighter plane before its final landing on Niʻi-hau. What was left smoldered slowly, threatening explosion but not capable of the feat.

Howard did not know about the attack that took place earlier that morning on Oahu and Pearl Harbor. Neither did any of the other inhabitants of the isolated island of Niʻihau, the westernmost of the eight main islands that make up the Hawaiian archipelago.

Their only contact with the outside world came in the form of weekly visits from the owner and foreman of the island, Alymer Robinson. That, and a hand held radio that was located within the farmhouse.

The villagers began arriving at the scene of the crash and assisted Howard in getting the pilot safely away from the wreckage.

That was the custom in Niʻihau, as they were thoughtful people. Often caring about others more than they cared about themselves.

Their care showed in the concern on their faces as they eyed the visitor who arrived out of the sky that morning.

Most of the villagers of Ni'ihau had lived there all of their lives. They were there to work the land for the family that had bought it 77 years prior.

The island of Ni'ihau was sold to Elizabeth McHutcheson Sinclair in 1864 for $10,000 in gold bars and a baby grand piano to seal the sale.

The deal for the island was made by Sinclair with King Kamehameha IV, who had a very difficult pandemic to deal with at the time he decided to sell the island and for the most part, the inhabitants that lived there.

The arrangement was one that solidified the history of that island and its people for 77 years. On that fateful day in 1941, the island of Ni'ihau had a population of 161 souls who called the second oldest of the Hawaiian islands home.

Howard and the villagers who were streaming in, took the pilot into the shade.

They talked for a second about what they should do with this man.

"Who is he?" One asked.

"Where did he come from?" Another said.

"What does he want from us?" A woman pondered.

Howard knew that many on the island had heard the plane crash and he knew they would come looking for the plane and would see it for themselves like many had already done.

There was no hiding this from the people and he decided it best to take the man to the village and let the people decide what should be done with the Japanese man.

Howard recognized the insignia on the plane as that of the Japanese and he was also aware of the recent oil embargo the United States had enacted on the island nation of Japan that stood to the west of Niʻihau some 3,784 miles.

"This can be no good," he said aloud to the others. "We need to take him to the village and we will decide what to do with him then and there."

Ben Kanehale was a master at sheering sheep and was accustomed to throwing the animals on his shoulders as a means of transporting them from one place to another. He had grown large as a man, working for the Robinson family in this capacity. Ben was looked at as a leader of the village, not only because of his size but also for the way he'd worked his way up in standing within the Robinson family and community. He and his wife had made a life on the small island and visitors tended to make him nervous.

There was no way around this and any uninvited guest would have to be brought into the eye of the village. Ben knew this was the only way. He put the little pilot on his big shoulders with Howard and the others watching.

Howard felt he was responsible for the pilot now having found him the way he had. Ben assured Howard after a few protestations that he would make sure a solution was found for this visitor.

"We will do it the right and pono way, Howard," Ben said in Hawaiian to him, whom he had known most of his life. "Like we have always done and will always do."

This principle had been instilled in Ben's very being since the day he came into this earth. His elder, or kupuna had made sure he was taught this as a young man and carried it with him everywhere he went in life.

The pilot slowly came back to reality on the walk to the village. At first, consciousness came back to him like a trickle. Soon it came back to him all at once like a flood.

"Where are you taking me?" the pilot asked Ben Kanehale in Japanese. "Take me back to my plane. Take me back to my plane, or I will kill you and all of you. There is a submarine coming to rescue me and they will surely end you if you do not release me and return to me what is mine."

The pilot tried to reach for his pistol but only felt the emptiness of where it once rested.

The pilot squirmed like a baby who didn't want to be held. Ben readjusted to the movements with his tremendous strength and squeezed the will right out of Shige who soon learned that resistance in this capacity would be fruitless.

Ben wouldn't respond to the pilot's incessant pleas to be put down in Japanese. In response, he started to chant traditional Hawaiian songs taught through the years by his elders. It helped him to calm his mind and focus on the task at hand.

"We will have to take him to the Haradas," Howard said to Ben. "They will be able to speak his language and find out what he is doing here."

"Before we bother them, let us summon the old man. He will be able to understand the language he speaks and he will better be able to understand what it is he wants from us on this island that we all call home," Ben said in response.

The pilot found the Hawaiians to be annoying and against the general war effort of his country. He viewed this man who was carrying him as an enemy that had to be dealt with.

He would have his revenge on the huge Hawaiian who had brought him shame.

The unlikely trio walked instep with many following behind, now nearing the village of Pu'uwai. It was the only village on the island.

They began to slow their pace in anticipation of the explanation that would be needed for the haole who was in their presence. They would have to try and explain something they did not know the cause of, or why it had happened.

Shige again began to protest against his captors and let them know in Japanese the vengeance that would be taken on them for interfering with his official duties. Word was sent to gather the Harradas and to call for the old man who spoke Japanese.

The villagers marveled at the pilot and his clothing as they wondered what he was doing there.

"Send for Ishimatsu Shintani, the island bookkeeper," Howard said to the crowd. "He speaks this man's language and will be the best to understand what it is he wants from us and this island. He is from Japan and was not born in Hawai'i, so he is the best at this job we have for him."

With that, the villagers tracked down the old man who hadn't lived in Japan since he was a young man. He came to the mad scene and looked around at all the villagers gathered around the pilot Shige.

"What is it that you want me to do?" Ishimatsu asked of Howard, who stood over the seated pilot.

"We want you to talk to him in your native tongue and figure out what it is that he wants from us and why it is that he has come here," Howard said to the old man. "That is why we have called for you today. This and nothing more."

Ishimatsu looked at the seated pilot and greeted him in the traditional Japanese way.

"Why is it that you have come to this island and what do you want?" The old man asked the young pilot plainly.

"We have come to destroy the American fleet in Pearl Harbor and we succeeded in doing just that this morning. My plane was damaged and I crash landed here. A submarine will be here to rescue me and deal with any who have treated me badly and not assisted in the Japanese victory."

The look on Ishimatsu's face soured and he did not respond to Shige's announcement of what it was he was doing on the island of Ni`i-hau.

Ishimatsu was a strict man, and fearing the truth behind the pilot's words, he knew that trouble would follow this announcement. He would go to his house and head up to the highest peaks of the island to avoid what was coming.

"What is it that he told you?" Howard asked of Ishimatsu.

The old man did not bother to respond and simply walked away from the village. He went straight to his house and gathered the essentials he would need to camp out until the trouble had passed away. He loaded up his donkey and was up the hillside by late afternoon.

The villagers were left dumbfounded by the response Ishimatsu had to the pilot. It left them confused and they quickly sought out Yoshio Harada and his wife Irene.

While a party was sent to locate the Haradas, who were of Japanese descent and could speak the language, the villagers went about treating Shige as a guest of honor. They put together an impromptu luau for the pilot and gave him a feast that he would not soon forget.

"We make war on these people and they return the favor with pineapple and smoked pig," Shige said to Howard in his native tongue, in between bites of succulent pork that was the best he had ever tasted.

Howard looked at Shige, feasting and smiling. Howard couldn't place the mistrust he felt in his heart, but he knew that something wasn't right with this visitor, who in the Hawaiian tongue would be called a Haole, or "one without breath" as it translates to in English.

Leis with fragrant flowers were presented to Shige and he acknowledged the generosities with a smile. It had been one of the best and worst days of his life, rolled into one singular spectacular day. He feared for his life at many points throughout the course of the day and was convinced that it would be his last, only to live through the ordeal to be treated to an authentic Hawaiian lua for attacking the neighbor island earlier in the morning,

Shige knew that things would become violent at some point on this island. There would be lots of violence from here on out and there was nothing anyone could do to change that now. He knew that some of the people in the village would have to pay the price for the final victory.

Shige didn't care some of these people in the village would have to die if he were to make it back to the carrier. To him, that was part of the price that had to be paid in order for Japan to gain the ultimate victory.

The decision was made by the village after talking with the Haradas that the pilot should be put under their care. It was also decided that the Harada's house would be placed under guard by Hawaiians armed with spears and knives. This was meant to be a precaution against any possible trouble that might come from the uninvited guest, either intended or unintended.

It wasn't usual business on the island of Ni'ihau for such things to take place, and even more unusual for the residents to take the precaution of arming themselves. This was a topic that was talked about by every resident of the island in a short time as rumors circulated about the uninvited guest who had made his way into their lives.

Most of them couldn't comprehend the amount of damage that had been inflicted on the island of Oahu that day. Many of the villagers had never before been off the island of Ni'ihau, and any other place seemed strange and dangerous to them.

The pilot, however, knew full well the damage that had been dealt to the American Navy. He also knew there was a response coming from Japan's new enemy and that they would be prepared to counter anything that came their way. The Japanese had been preparing for this fight for a long time. Now that it had arrived, there was nothing that was going to scare them away from the fight that lay ahead.

The villagers led the strange new man to the Harradas and made sure the guards were briefed on what they needed to do. One by one, the villagers left out of sight of the Harada's house wondering what would become of the pilot.

The Harradas

Shige waited until the villagers had left them and until the guards started to fall asleep before he began to speak with the Harradas, who were thrilled to have another Japanese-speaking person staying in their humble house.

"Do you know what has happened today?" Shige said to the Harradas, who were serving their guest some tea.

"We have only one radio on the island," Yoshio Harada answered the pilot. Yoshio's wife remained silent and went about her work indiscriminately.

"We attacked the United States Navy this morning at Pearl Harbor. I saw with my own eyes, the billowing smoke that poured out of the battleships. I saw with my own eyes the complete destruction of the American fleet on the island of Oahu. The empire is now at war with the Americans after this attack."

Yoshio Harrada, and his wife Irene, contemplated this information presented to them for a moment before Yoshio responded.

"Do you think the empire will come to Ni`ihau?" Yoshio asked of Shige.

"They will most certainly come to rescue me," he responded. "This island was designated as the crash landing location for any planes damaged in the attack. And when they do come, they will show lethal force and kill anyone who tries to resist. It's clear Japan is going to win this war. The way the attack unfolded today showed us this clear as the morning sky."

"How do you know this?" Yoshio asked of the pilot.

"They were not prepared for the attack today and it cost them their entire fleet. There is no way they can recover in time to fight off the Japanese Navy. It's just a matter of time now before their navy is overrun and they are forced to surrender."

Yoshio and Irene looked at each other, neither speaking but communicating in a way that people who have been married for a long time often do.

"If what you say is true, then we must remain loyal to the country of our family origin," Yoshio said to Shige, who had finished his tea and gave a gesture of thanks to Irene. "We were not born in Japan you see? We are merely Japanese descendants and for the most part, this country has been good to us."

"That will change after today," Shige responded, cutting Yoshio off. "They will certainly be hostile to all Japanese after the attack today. If you are loyal to this country, they will repay it by imprisoning you for the color of your skin as they have done so many times. The goal of this war is to break free of their rule and influence in the Pacific and create a new destiny for all of Japan and our people. If you are loyal to Japan as a Japanese descendant when Japan needs, she will be loyal to you when the time comes to collect your reward for such loyalty."

Yoshio and Irene exchanged nervous looks before the wife asked her guest, "What is it that you will have us do for the empire of Japan?"

"You know this island and have lived here for a long time," Shige responded. "What I need is for you to help me retrieve what has been taken from me and the empire of Japan."

"And what has been taken from you and the empire?" Yoshio asked.

"When my warplane crashed, I was relieved of my papers and maps of Oahu. Also, my pistol was taken from my side. There is important information in these papers that must not fall into the wrong hands."

Yoshio stared blankly at Shige, thinking about what role he should play in this trouble.

"My wife and I live a peaceful life here," he responded. "We have never been in a situation on this island where the village decided that someone should be put under the kuleana of a guard. This shows the people here are really unsure of what is to be done with you. I hear what you say to my wife and me and we know that if we helped you, we would be going against this village and the people we have lived and worked with for years now."

The pilot shrugged his shoulders and resigned himself to wait the situation out until it reached a conclusion. He did not know how, when, or what the resolution would look like, but he was sure that the day was coming to an end. It was a relief to see the end to a day he though he might not live to see the end of. He felt a sense of accomplishment knowing that he lived through the day and would live to see another.

It was a day that had seen a glorious victory for Japan and a personal defeat that saw him deserted on the forbidden island.

He reiterated to himself over and over he would make it off of the island and one day return to his home island once again.

This thought brought him comfort as he faded into a light sleep, churning through the events that occured that day in his mind.

Time Marches on

The inhabitants of Ni'ihau waited for the steward of the land to come and make things right. They believed they would be relieved the day after the uninvited guest arrived in his warplane. But Alymer Robinson did not come. The residents could not understand why. Alymer was never late.

Seeking answers to why this uninvited visitor showed up to their island the way he did, Ben Kanehele and his wife began searching for answers.

They approached Harold and asked him if he knew where the old battery-operated radio he once had was.

Harold, still absorbing all that had happened in a short amount of time, was pleased to help in any way he could.

He quickly produced the radio and fresh batteries were obtained in a haste to make it functional. They turned the radio on and a broadcast began.

"Good evening, ladies and gentlemen, I am speaking to you tonight at a very serious moment in our history. The Cabinet is convening and the leaders in Congress are meeting with the President. The State Department and Army and Navy officials have been with the President all afternoon. In fact, the Japanese ambassador was talking to the president at the very time that Japan's airships were bombing our citizens in Hawaii and the Philippines and sinking one of our transports loaded with lumber on its way to Hawaii.

By tomorrow morning the members of Congress will have a full report and be ready for action.

In the meantime, we the people are already prepared for action. For months now the knowledge that something of this kind might happen has been hanging over our heads and yet it seemed impossible to believe, impossible to drop the everyday things of life and feel that there was only one thing which was important - preparation to meet an enemy no matter where he struck. That is all over now and there is no more uncertainty.

We know what we have to face and we know that we are ready to face it.

I should like to say just a word to the women in the country tonight. I have a boy at sea on a destroyer, for all I know he may be on his way to the Pacific. Two of my children are in coast cities on the Pacific. Many of you all over the country have boys in the services who will now be called upon to go into action. You have friends and families in what has suddenly become a danger zone. You cannot escape anxiety. You cannot escape a clutch of fear at your heart and yet I hope that the certainty of what we have to meet will make you rise above these fears.

We must go about our daily business more determined than ever to do the ordinary things as well as we can and when we find a way to do anything more in our communities to help others, to build morale, to give a feeling of security, we must do it. Whatever is asked of us I am sure we can accomplish it. We are the free and unconquerable people of the United States of America.

To the young people of the nation, I must speak a word tonight. You are going to have a great opportunity. There will be high moments in which your strength and your ability will be tested. I have faith in you. I feel as though I was standing upon a rock and that rock is my faith in my fellow citizens.

Now we will go back to the program we had arranged..."

They connected the arrival of Shige with the attack and knew war had now descended upon the islands and the nation they were a territory of.

The startled Hawaiians confronted Shige at the Harada's house, coming together as a group. They meant to get answers from the man as to why he was really there and why he had not made it known what had happened to him earlier that day.

"Yoshio, we want to know why he has come to make war on us and the haoles," Ben Kanehale said as he and the group brandishing torches approached the house.

Yoshio spoke to Shige, and they decided it was best if Yoshio tell the villagers what he had already told the Haradas.

"Japan and the United States are now at war as of this morning," Yoshio said. "This pilot was one of many that launched an attack on the U.S. Navy in Oahu. Many people died. His plane was damaged and he could not make it back to the carrier, so he landed here as he was instructed to do if their planes were damaged."

The news did not come as a shock to them as much as it had when they heard it on the radio. Shige came out of the house and they all looked at him with the new knowledge of what he was a part of and why he had come to their island.

That night, the villagers went to Pleho Beach and started the biggest fire they could muster to signal the duress they were under. They expected Alymer Robinson to arrive the next day as he did once a week, but they wanted to make sure he knew there was trouble.

Five guards remained at the Harrada's house as the family and Shige became more familiar with each other's plight in life.

"The day is coming where you will have to

make your choice, Yoshio Harrada," said Shige that morning. "You were not born in Japan, but you have Japanese ancestry. The blood of Japan flows in you. You have an obligation to make the right choice in this decision. Japan is going to win this war. The United States is crippled after the attack on Pearl Harbor and they will not be able to stand against the Japanese Navy."

Shige pushed the hope of rescue down inside himself like the thought of how many he knew died the day of the attack. As each day had passed, he lost hope of a submarine coming to retrieve him from his plight.

Shige didn't feel the need to share his hopes of rescue.

The Harradas were tied to a deep feeling of an obligation to the villagers to look after Shige. They felt torn in their loyalty towards the nation they were residents of and the nation their forefathers had come from. In one regard, Yoshio Harrada felt the pride of earning the right to be called an American citizen, but on the other a bitter sting of prejudice and hate towards his family and himself on account of his heritage.

Yoshio Harrada had felt how the American dream can be a dangerous thing as well as a blessing. The blessings had taken many forms for himself and the prejudice twice as many. The island had offered him the chance to escape all that and live in a way that pleased himself and his wife.

Yoshio weighed the option before him like a man calculating what is best for his family with the knowledge he had at his disposal.

Alymer Robinson waited as patiently as the good lord could afford him nearby on the island of Kaua`i. He was told by the United States Navy that ships would not be allowed to cross the Kaulakahi Channel until further notice. Even to get to his property. This didn't sit well with the man.

"The residents of Ni`ihau are like beautifully ignorant children," he told the Navy commander who placed the no travel restriction. Alymer was sure to talk to the man who made the order directly. "They may be in danger and need help. If I cannot attend to the residents on our land and the government can offer no assistance, who will attend to their needs?"

The officer, cold and calculated in his orders refuted the request despite Alymer's consternation.

It was clear at the moment travel to the island of Ni`ihau from Kaua`i would be impossible for the time being until the Navy lifted their no travel ban.

With the new routine that had found the Harradas and Shige, they found lots of time to talk and plan. Soon the plan became reality as Shige convinced Yoshio Harrada that his pistol and documents were his property and needed to be returned to him.

Yoshio, afraid at his assertion these items needed to be returned, asked for help from Ishimatsu Shintani, who was Alymer's bookkeeper. Ishimatsu visited the Harradas and Shige upon receiving an invitation to come and speak with them, which Yoshio had delivered personally.

"We need to convince Howard to return the pistol and documents to Shige," Yoshio informed Ishimatsu Shintani, who shook his head when hearing this. "I'm not interested in finding any trouble here. I've lived in peace on this island for a long time and I hope I live here long after he leaves this place," Ishimatsu said indignantly.

"I understand what he says about the war and what happened in Pearl Harbor. I can't stand to think of helping the enemy when the outcome of this conflict is still undecided."

The bookkeeper looked at the pilot and measured his response, anticipating the outcome of what he was going to say.

Shige took his time, clearing his throat before he began to speak.

"The outcome of this war was decided on December, 7th when I watched the American fleet burn and sink into the ocean. Today is December 10th. There has been nobody here to check on the people of Ni'ihau."

The pilot let that fact sink in before continuing on. All eyes in the room were on him.

"If they truly cared for these people, they would have been here to see if they were ok," Shige said, relishing the simple truth.

"It's hard to say, but you have a point. If they really cared, they would do more for these people than they do," Yoshio added, trying to help convince the old man of what had to be done.

"You two have decided that this is something that I must do?" said the bookkeeper.

"Harold respects you. You two know each other and he will surely listen to you and the request to return what is not his," Yoshio Harrada said to the old man.

"He may respect me and knows me, but if he refuses to do what you ask of him, what am I to do?" Ishimatsu said quizzically. "Howard is a man of his own ordering and he will do what he thinks is best for the island and the people of Ni'ihau. I can tell you that he thought the items something of a threat, or he would not have taken them from the pilot."

The men shared a collective moment of silence, broken only by the insistence of Shige that his missing items be returned by any means necessary.

"These items do not belong to the man and I demand that he return what is mine and Japan's," Shige said, his seriousness reiterating.

"What will you do once the items are returned to you?" Ishimatsu asked the pilot solemnly. "Will there be trouble that follows once you have these things you want from Howard?"

"Only if he denies what is mine will there be trouble," Shige said to the old man. "If he denies giving me what is mine, then there will surely be trouble."

Ishimatsu agreed to do what the two men were asking him. Not out of what he viewed as a betrayal, but as a service to the island and the residents to try and resolve the situation with as little trouble as possible.

In the back of Ishimatsu's mind was the assertion the pilot had made that there would be no trouble if the items were returned to him. He held the pilot at his word and believed his promise there would be no trouble if the pistol and the papers were returned to him.

Ishimatsu feared what would happen if Howard refused to return the items. He also feared reporting back the news that he had failed to convince Howard to Yoshio and Shige.

He went to his humble house where he had lived for many years and sought out the hidden can he kept in the floorboards, holding all the money he had saved in his adult life. A wad of bills added up to a total of $200.

He would gladly give it all to Howard in exchange for the papers and gun Howard had taken from the pilot. It was a matter of grave circumstance and an easy exchange in his mind. After all, the money was just paper and it could be replaced. The lives that could be lost in the trouble to come could never be replaced and would change the island forever. He did not want to see that happen to his home.

Ishimatsu rolled a cigarette and smoked it slowly, exhaling his thoughts in a swirling cloud of smoke.

"If Howard doesn't take what I am offering him in exchange for what the pilot wants, then I will leave to the hills and wait this situation out. It would be safer up there and you could see anyone who wanted to make trouble here on this island and avoid them."

The old man thought these things over as the stars spilled out into the night one at a time until they flowed like a silent river across the stretched out black canvas of a sky. His thoughts left him confused and anxious, but ready to try and keep any trouble from coming that wasn't necessary.

That was the way he had seen things like this blow over in the past. This is the approach he would take and making up his mind brought a calming peace to him.

Pilikia

The old man prepared everything for both outcomes.

If Harold were to accept the money he would offer him for the papers and the revolver to be returned, then he would be out the money. He would take a loss on that outcome, but he would gain the loss of trouble.

With the items returned, Shige had no need to inflict trouble on the people of the island.

If Harold decided there was no amount of money in this world to change his mind, then the people would be open to the pilikia, or trouble that would come their way.

The old man knew very well the outcome riding on his attempt to get Harold to do something other than what his will told him to do.

A feeling in his gut told him there was nothing he could do to change the outcome. He felt even worse for trying to do something for Japan when he had not been there since he was a boy.

The man took some time in his thoughts before loading up his belongings onto the half horse, half mule he used for work and traveling the island. Gentle strokes on the animal's head were given to reassure it as the began leaving home. These things were not easy to do for the old bookkeeper.

There had been many strange happenings in his lifetime he had borne witness to, but things were changing more rapidly now on this earth and island than he had ever known before. The pilot was a sign of the time the old man thought to himself. It was surely an indicator that things would never be the same on the island and in the world.

"This is just another sign that the old times are dead and with it, the old people like me who are left. We are the lone defenders of the way things once were. There is no care anymore for the way things were once done," he said to himself while riding to Harold to propose a way to avoid the lurking trouble.

Ishimatsu had packed for two outcomes, and the second outcome required packing for an extended stay out in the bush. He was familiar with the way of the land and how to survive out in it as he had lived most of his life and all of his adult life on the island of Nii'hau. It was like a family member to him and he knew exactly what was needed in order to make it out in the wild here. It did not scare him to do what he must, but the thought of being forced into a wilderness exile did scare him.

The feeling in his gut intensified to the point where he put some rice in it to ease the butterflies that flapped deep within.

"Harold is a reasonable man, but he believes in what is right. I think he believes that he is protecting the island by relieving the pilot of his belongings, but it might just be the kind of thing that causes more trouble than it avoids," Ishimatsu thought to himself as he came upon the wreckage of the plane Shige had guided to that destined place.

Seeing the plane gave new meaning to the task before Ishimatsu as he gazed at the plane in its sad state, thinking how all this misfortune could have been avoided in the first place.

"There's no point in thinking any of those thoughts as this is where the plane came to a rest," he thought. "Now all that can be helped is how this entire thing plays out."

Harold's humble abode was not far from the wreckage, and Ishimatsu wished that Shige had landed close to his house so this whole thing could have been different. He had to remind himself again that was not the way of it and there was no point in wanting things to be different as it only took away from what had to be done.

Ishimatsu arrived at his destination to find Harold sitting on his front lanai, cleaning the pistol he had retrieved from Shige when he was half conscious.

"Luck is a funny thing, Harold," Ishimatsu said to him. "One minute we have nothing, and the next providence has laid before us the key to our salvation and we often don't know it?"

"If you have come to try and retrieve what was taken from the pilot, you will not succeed in your endeavor I'm afraid Ishimatsu," Harold said instinctually. "There is nothing you can offer me that will dissuade me from keeping what I found off of that Japanese man. I must keep it. If he has it, he will surely do harm to you, me, and this island. Of that I am sure."

"Harold, he has assured me there will be no trouble if his possessions are returned to him," Ishimatsu paused to let this sink in. "I fear what he will do if his possessions are not returned to him. He has a duty to uphold, Harold. If he does not get back what has been taken from him, he will do harm to you in order to retrieve his possessions. This I am certain of, Harold."

Harold finished cleaning the pistol in his hands and gazed at it intently for a moment, as if the pistol was a key to the future. He shook his head.

"This pistol is not his any longer as he was an unwelcomed visitor to our island and lost it in his entry to this place," Harold stood up from his resting position to look into Ishimatsu's eyes. "If he had this pistol, what's to keep him from using it? You are a wise old man and I am sure you have thought this thing over and there is a reason why you have all your things packed onto your animal. Why have you taken the trouble to come here to me and at the same time, pack your things for pilikia?"

"Harold, you know the importance of this. You have known me for the better part of your life and I come here out of respect for that knowing of each other," Ishimatsu's face reflected the authenticity of his statement. "You know that I have come here out of respect for you and all that live on this island in relative peace. That peace is now threatened by our uninvited guest, but war has come to this place and is coming more. I fear that if we do not abide by the wishes of this pilot, those wishes will become violent and may end the lives of some of those living on this island. If not for now, but maybe down the line. Do you wish to have the blood of those that will be affected by your decision on your hands? Harold, I come to you out of the wisdom of an old man looking to keep that from happening. If you refuse what I am asking of you, I will understand and resign myself to the company of the bush."

Harold looked the old man over, seeing if his words were made out of love or fear. He could see that he was trembling and that he was not happy about the decision that had to be made. Harold dared not show the fear that began to spread over his conscious coldly.

"I thank you for your wisdom and consideration, Ishimatsu. You have always been a resolute man and we all respect you for that, but I must refuse your request," Harold told him. "Not out of disagreement for what you are asking, but out of fear for the island just as yourself. However, I do not want to act out of fear, but out of courage for what has to be done here. Alymer will be here before long, and I will turn the gun over to the owner of the land. Even if we don't agree that the land is rightfully the Robinsons to own, we must agree that it is not for the Japanese to decide who gets to have guns in this place of relative peace. We both came here to work for the Robinson's and that is what I intend to keep doing, long after this man has left this island. I will not let him or Japan jeopardize a single Hawaiian. I understand that you are from Japan and have some empathy for this boy, but when it comes down to it, he or his nation will not have that same empathy for you my friend. We must rid ourselves of any responsibility in assisting them in any way."

The old man smiled at Harold with the knowledge that comes with experience, for he knew the decision might cost Harold his life. But with the wisdom of his age, he knew that the only choice he could control was that of his own making. And he would choose now to leave for the safety of nature and find refuge in it.

He said a silent prayer for the safety of Harold and for that of the village. He left for the sanctuary and peace of the wilderness, a place he knew he would be safe until Alymer and the rest returned to make sure that there wouldn't be any more trouble. From his roost in the highest spot of the island, he could see the bonfires that had burned for four nights, beckoning help from Kaua'i.

Harold went back to the village of Pu'uwai and stored the pistol for safekeeping near the lone shotgun on the island in an old warehouse, and then went to his house and retrieved the pilot's papers from the hiding spot in his wall.

Harold examined the aerial maps of Pearl Harbor and all the foreign attack plans, attempting to understand them as if he were reading a newspaper.

Yoshio and Shige waited for Ishimatsu to return as expected. As the hours rolled on, they expected he had failed in his task to persuade Harold.

"Yoshio, the time has come for us to act on what we know and what we know must happen. We cannot expect, or count on anyone else to do what we must now take on ourselves to do."

Yoshio, looking at his wife Irene, knew what it was Shige meant.

"Is there nothing else to be done then, Shige?"

"I'm afraid it is solely up to you and me now to make this wrong right. We must also do what we have to for Japan. There will be no making things right now. They will be made right only through war and the acts of war that are to follow," Shige said with a tone of authority.

"You both will end up dead," Irene Harada said to the pair. "They are too many for the two of you to fight as a whole. They will eventually overcome you out of sheer numbers alone."

"Don't let your wife dissuade you Yoshio from what you have to do," Shige said to the husband and wife. "She will not pay what is owed when Japan wins this war and what you failed to do lives with you for the rest of your life. Think about your future. Where will your wife be when this is all over?"

Irene looked at her husband Yoshio, already knowing the choice her husband was to make. She knew him better than he knew himself. She could see the time reaching into eternity that would be spent without him. She felt the presence of the love of her life leave her while standing before her like the breath that left her in the moment.

"My wife, you know that I have to help this man get what is his and Japan's," he said to Irene. "If I don't do this, we will be the worse for it. We may never be able to live with ourselves if I do not help him. He is but one here, and with me there is a chance."

Irene did not fight the feeling any longer after that moment, accepting the destiny that would come from this. She remained silent as the two went about planning Shige's escape from the guards and retrieving the pistol and papers that were taken from him by Harold.

"There is also a shotgun that is kept in the farmhouse by Alymer," Yoshio confessed to Shige. "It is hanging up on the wall and is there for the taking. It is the only other gun I know of that is on the island."

"We can take the guns off of the plane and set fire to it after we get them," Shige instructed. "That way we will have enough to hold the island if the need arises."

Yoshio in his eagerness to help Shige did not consider the fact that he may have to kill or harm those he had lived with for so long and who were so good to him and his wife Irene. As Irene listened to their plan develop, she could see all kinds of possibilities play out in her mind, ranging from peaceful resolution to tragedy.

Yoshio knew the first thing in the plan would involve breaking the guard and getting away from his house. This would be a simple task and the two would use the familiarity and trust that existed between the Yoshio's and the guards. To Shige, it was simple. They would use the thing that had been gifted to him as a weapon. Food.

"We must get your wife to distract the guards using food, Yoshio," Shige said to his co-conspirator. "If we can get them to focus on the food and not on where I am, then we can easily gain liberty and make our way to Harold and the pistol. Once we get that pistol, we can then go to the plane and get the machine guns from there. Once we get those, we will destroy the plane."

Shige felt a sense of responsibility in keeping his plane and his papers from falling into the hands of the enemy. In the papers Harold took from him, he knew there was much that the enemy could derive from them. These included maps, attack plans, and carrier locations, amongst other things. He knew the shame that would come on his family if he were the one who let these things fall into the hands of the enemy.

He did not care if he were to make it out of this alive. That hope had left him on the first day arriving on the island. Irene's fears were nothing but a probable reality to him and he did not fear them. He feared more the chance of his death being looked on as a failure to his country as something that haunted his conscious. The Haradas were meant to be here in his mind to help him accomplish the task of keeping the enemy from getting those papers. He would die fighting for this purpose and he knew by now that there was no submarine coming to rescue him.

He must do this and see it through and have the strength to do it well. This is what flooded his mind, and thoughts of when he was a boy in Japan preparing to take a test.

He felt as if he were that same boy now, but the test was in a different form. He longed for the nostalgia of the simpler times in his native land.

This test was too far from the simple comforts he longed for that seemed like distant dreams he had long ago woke from. The island of Ni`ihau was like no place he had imagined before, and not what he imagined Hawai`i to be in his imagination. The way these people lived was closer to tribal than any form of civilization he had ever seen in his life. They lived in a simple manner that he was unaccustomed to seeing on his home island, and he could not understand why this island was said to be uninhabited by his people. What were these people doing here living like this?

The anger of the misinformation was a frustration that boiled up inside of him, and he had lost the control switch. He urged Irene to cook the guards their favorite dish, which was a simple chicken dish she had made for them before.

When she was finished preparing the food, she took it to the guard who was fixed in front of the house. The other two guards had just left. It was around midday when the guards had lost interest in remaining at the same spot for so long. They wanted to be tending to their homes and business rather than play guard to this Japanese man who they did not know.

"Have some dinner, I know you are hungry," Irene said to the lone guard, handing him the dish she had prepared. "It's not easy being tasked with having to watch his every move. He doesn't move much and is fond of talking too much with my husband. What do you think will become of him?"

The guard took a bite of the chicken and rice, thinking before he answered.

"I think this will turn out how it has to turn, and most likely it will be something we don't see coming," the guard said to Irene. He finished his bowl before thanking her for the food.

Irene took out a phonograph and started to play some Japanese music.

The music was too loud for the liking of the lone guard as he went inside to see if Shige had finished eating.

He was not there to the shock of the guard. The guard frantically looked about the house, then ran outside where Irene was busying herself about the garden. She laughed silently, thinking about how easy it was to confuse the guard.

The men were quick about their task, attacking the lone guard from behind in his confusion. Shige knocked the guard unconscious with a piece of Koa wood, striking him on the back of the head.

The guard didn't scream out as the thud of the thick wood was the only sound made, despite the sound of the falling body of the man. The sound of the struggle was muffled by the music Irene was playing outside while she worked in the garden.

Yoshio and Shige took the unconscious guard and carried him to a warehouse directly down from the Harada house. They struggled to carry the heavy man, finally getting him inside the warehouse and tying him up to a post inside.

A 16-year-old boy who had by chance witnessed Shige and Yoshio carry the guard, stood outside the warehouse.

Shige approached the boy who had watched the scene unfold as Yoshio stayed inside the warehouse, retrieving the shotgun that was stored inside. He saw Shige's pistol had also been stored near the shotgun. He grabbed them both without delay, thinking much trouble had been avoided in finding the pistol.

Yoshio handed Shige the pistol, and he took the shotgun. They told the boy he would be coming with them, as Shige pointed the pistol at him and was not afraid to make an example of him. They started out with the boy in front of them, making their way to the crashed Zero.

Harold, who was in the outhouse nearby relieving himself, looked out to see the boy walking in front of Shige and Yoshio with his hands up. He saw the gun he had left in the warehouse for safekeeping in the hands of Shige.

Harold, who had just returned from meeting Ishimatsu, pulled his pants up and ran from the outhouse in the direction of the village.

Shige saw him out of the corner of his eye and fired a shot from his hip, narrowly missing Harold, who took cover behind an outcropping of rocks. Harold didn't wait as he continued running after he had gained cover.

The shot was heard by the villagers and they quickly discovered the guards and Shige were missing from the Harada's house.

Not missing the opportunity, Shige got in the plane and turned on the radio equipment. He made a few calls, asking for help and reporting the downed plane.

He waited for a response, but none came. The boy who had been taken prisoner noticed there was no response to the pilot's calls in Japanese, and he was thankful for that.

The stillness was interrupted by the sound of machine guns, as Shige fired the guns to see if they were damaged in the landing. The bullets ripped through the Kiawe bush, and the villagers were filled with even more terror as the sounds of war began to ravage the island.

The man who had been tasked with guarding Shige was dazed from the blow to the back of his head. He removed his constraints after some struggle and gained his liberty. He went outside of the warehouse to find the gathered villagers and he told his story of how he was taken prisoner by the pilot and Yoshio.

In fear, most of the villagers fled without delay, taking to the bush, caves, and the distant beaches of the island. They would rather wait until help arrived than try and face the armed pilot themselves. It was a matter of self-preservation and the calculation was simple for most, and they made a decision.

Shige continued looking inside the Zero to see if there was anything he could use to help take the Hawaiians prisoner. The papers were not stashed within the plane, but they had enough ammunition in the machine guns to kill every person on the island.

Shige forced the boy to help him remove the machine guns and the ammunition as they loaded it into a nearby cart, with the guns and ammunition separated into two different carts.

The first machine gun would not budge. No matter how hard the boy, Yoshio, and Shige moved it in all directions, the gun was stuck. It was stuck fast when the landing crunched it into a position where it was impossible to remove without the use of machinery.

The second machine gun proved to be the best option, as they removed it within a half hour. They were not bothered while they did their tasks as the sound of the guns did enough to keep all away.

The guards who were ordered to watch the house of the Haradas felt as though he had let his village down. He reported to Harold who had just got to the village, and Ben Kanehale, that Shige and Yoshio had left their guard.

Harold knew they would go to his house to retrieve the pilot's papers. He didn't know that the Japanese had ordered their pilots not to let the papers fall into enemy hands. He knew now that the old man knew this, or knew it intuitively.

It became clear to him in an instant what he must do now, and so without hesitation, he began to gather up a group of the remaining villagers to row to Kauai.

"It's apparent Alymer is not allowed to sail here, as we have had a fire every night for four nights and have not heard from them in any way, so we must go there before the pilot returns to seek his vengeance for himself and his country. Once we get to Kaua'i's western shores, we can get to Alymer and tell him what has happened here. He will be able to help us and bring help here, for we do not have the means to fight off any kind of invasion, however small."

"Who will stay then, Harold?" asked Ben Kanehale. "Some of us will have to stay as a diversion. If all of us go, the pilot will know something is up and he will get desperate. My wife and I will stay behind while you seek help."

They talked amongst themselves, deciding who would go to Kaua'i and who would stay. Those who were going totaled six, as Ben Kanehale and others who were staying prepared those who were to row across the channel what to expect.

They all went down to Kiekie from the village Puuwai. They walked down the dirt road together in unison, preparing for the tasks to come.

They looked to the clear skies and stars for guidance through the night to come and the water looked relatively calm for a December evening.

They would have to row north around the tip of the island and around Lehua Rock in order to catch the current going east across the 17-mile channel to the Westside of Kaua'i.

"You are facing rowing for over ten hours nonstop, and once you get there, they may be prepared for war, so when you land, be careful to tell them who you are and where you are coming from," Ben Kanehale said to Harold. "And please do not forget us here as we will need you to make your journey and send help for us. Hopefully, we can keep Yoshio and this man within reason, but if things get worse, we will try and make it out just as you have."

The five who were to sail to Kaua'i and those who were to remain said their solemn goodbyes. One by one they loaded onto the inflatable boat they prepared that would serve as their vessel across the Kaulakahi Channel.

The men rowed in unison as they became smaller and smaller against the horizon to the gathered crowd seeing them off.

Ben Kanehale later went to the plane and found the carts with the ammunition and guns unguarded. He took the ammunition cart and ran it under cover to the beach and hid it where he hoped Shige and Yoshio would never find it. He made sure it was hidden under palm fronds and obstructed from sight, so anyone looking for it would have to remove the branches to find the ammunition.

This was something he could do to try and protect the villagers and the island. The only other thing he could do was kill the pilot, and he knew it might come to that as he looked up at the Decmeber moon above. Ben reflected on the day and what tomorrow may bring before he went back home to his wife, and was thankful they had each other to see this through.

An Act of War

Ben Kanehale and his wife Ella returned to the village of Puuwai to find an uneasy quiet. Ben couldn't shake the feeling he had made a mistake not leaving the island when he had the chance.

It was early night and the cool trade winds shook the palm trees gently, revealing the blanket of stars covering the sky. There was peace in the fact they were on their home island and this would play out in the place they knew so well. Ben was the leader of this place outside of the Robinsons, or so he felt.

He felt a strong stewardship tied to the island and he did not want to leave his home at the mercy of a foreigner. He had worked too hard in his life for too little. This little village was all he had in the world and he would be damned to see all that work and love he put into the place be destroyed. For better, or for worse, he had made his decision.

His wife, Ella, felt the same as her husband. There was nowhere for them to go if they left the island. This was their home and they had to make a stand. They had always got along with Yoshio and they hoped he would have mercy on them for that simple fact. Ella did not think Yoshio would do them harm when it came down to it, so she was resolute in her commitment to staying as her husband was.

Yoshio and Shige, with the machine gun taken from the plane, had tried to use the radio to contact the Japanese fleet multiple times.

"It's useless," Shige said to Yoshio. "They are not responding. There must be radio silence on this frequency now."

They set fire to the Zero, watching it burn, knowing there was no going back now. Smoke filled the sky as they left the burning plane behind, moving quickly to the nearby house of Harold. They found the door unlocked and they turned it inside out looking for the papers.

Shige looked at Harold's things, trying to get a picture inside the mind of the man he must now find. It was the last thing he needed to accomplish before there could be an end. And then when he had solved the last problem... well, that did not matter to him. It would work out how it had to at that point in time, but the thing that mattered the most, he would not fail in achieving.

"How do we find Harold, Yoshio?" Shige asked. "He must be somewhere on this small island. There are not many places to hide."

"We can make the others look for him," Yoshio said, knowing that he would have to do the thing that he feared the most to begin with. There was no other way. "They will know where he has gone to and we will find him. It is just a matter of time before the owner of the land is here, and when he comes, he will come with others. There is no doubt in my mind that the moment is coming closer by the minute. What will we do when that moment comes?"

"We will know what to do when that moment comes," Shige said. "I have called the fleet for help. They know that we are here, so they can come to our aid. We have to get those papers and keep them from falling into the hands of the U.S."

They were solidified in their endeavor as one. After tearing Harold's house to pieces in search of the papers that contained the valuable information, they set the house on fire, illuminating the last darkness of the night as morning crept forward.

Without delay, the two went into the silent village of Pu'uwai silhouetted by the fires they left behind, finding the Kanehales there, along with a few others who had concentrated in the streets.

"We don't want to kill you," Yoshio said to the people he had lived with and who had taken him in as a foreigner. "He just wants the papers that have been taken from him and his country. We have offered to buy the papers from Harold and he refused. The pilot is demanding his things back and he will not stop at killing every one of you in order to get the papers back. So, please help me in getting the papers back so nothing more has to happen here. We have all lived together for some time and you know me. We will let you all go once the papers are returned."

Ben Kanehale looked at his wife. They had known this moment would come and they would not give up the fact that Harold was on his way with the papers on a boat to Kaua'i.

"We will help you find Harold, he can't have gone far," Ben said to Yoshio and Shige, who angrily looked at the husband and wife. "He probably is in the hills with Ishimatsu. We will need to go before Alymer returns. He is due back at any time."

"If you are so sure of where he is, then there should be no problem with us keeping your wife until you return with Howard and the papers," Yoshio said as Shige listened, but could not understand what they were saying.

Ben looked at his wife Ella, her soft features trapped by the fate of the moment. His plan had ended inside himself before it had even started.

"She knows this island better than anyone here," Ben said. "I need her to help me find Harold as she also knows where he likes to go. Without her, I will not be able to find him as quickly, if at all."

Yoshio communicated what Ben had said to him in Japanese as Ben and Ella talked quietly in each others ear. Ben reassured her that everything would be ok and that he would return for her before long. She urged him not to leave her with the two men.

"I don't know what they will do at this point and I am an easy victim here without my husband," she said to him. Ben knew this and silently acknowledged his wife's concern.

"I will not spend long before I return to you. I promise," he said to Ella. "You can use your charm on them to try and talk them down from what they want to do and offer them a way out. This will buy us a little more time."

Shige looked at Ella after Yoshio had finished telling him that Ben was to look for Harold. Shige looked at the tall Hawaiian, seeing an enemy that he did not want to have to fight without the aid of the guns. He remained ready to pull it at any hint of a charge, and the thought had crossed Ben's mind.

"Let him go, and if he deceives us, we will kill his wife," Shige said to Yoshio in Japanese. "Make sure this is known to him to keep him from wasting our time."

"Will you kill her if he cannot find Harold?" Yoshio asked.

"If that is what needs to be done in order to get those papers, I will stop at nothing short," he said.

Yoshio looked at Ella, and then said, "As you wish, sir."

Ben and Ella hugged, and as Ben started

to head for the higher ground where he would pretend to look for Harold. Yoshio beckoned him to stop as he left and approached him.

"Ben, we have known each other for some time now and you have always been good to me before. Let me be good to you now and tell you that the pilot will kill your wife if you return empty-handed. I tell you this not as a threat, Ben Kanehale, but as a certainty. Please keep this in mind before you leave and if you know something about where Harold is, the time is now to tell us before you pay the ultimate price that can be paid."

Ben looked back at his wife and felt as if he had been in this moment before somewhere. He felt the moment was as familiar to him as something that had already happened. He just shook his head, knowing that he might have to kill the man he had come to know in order to save the life of his wife.

Ben and Kalima, who had also been taken by the pair on the road to Pu'uwai, went looking for Howard, knowing their plan was a farce.

"What should we do, Ben? They are surely halfway to Kaua'i by now," Kalima said, avoiding eye contact with Ben.

They stood there, looking out over the ridge towards Kaua'i, guessing at where the inflatable boat was in the night. The moon reflected off the ocean, illuminating the black water that reiterated they were alone in their task.

There was no help coming that night and they must turn back to Ella and the captors.

"We have to go back and tell them what has happened," Ben said to Kalima. "They will take their anger out on me for I have deceived them. They may try to kill me, but if they do I will fight them. You must be ready when that happens, Kalima."

They took some more time to gather their strength for what was to come. A trade wind carried in, fanning the palm leaves on the beaches down below the ridge. Ohi`a lehua trees lined the Upcountry, blooming red in the semi-annual flowering.

Ben remembered the story of the ohia lehua tree as he walked down from the Upcountry to face his fate. He had been told the story when he was a keiki, and it always stuck with him since his tuto told him it long ago.

Ohi`a was the strongest warrior of all the islanders of Hawaii. He was on the beach one day, pounding poi for his family and Lehau. Lehua was the most beautiful woman in all of Hawaii. Her beauty was renowned amongst all the people and Lehua had won her love.

While Ohi`a was laboring, pounding poi from the taro root, Pele observed him from afar. The goddess of creation and destruction was taken by Ohi`a, who stood seven feet tall, bristling with muscles and hidden only by a loincloth.

Pele approached Oh`ia and found that he had already pledged his love and life to Lehua, the sister of Pele.

Angered by this rejection, Pele turned the handsome warrior who was betrothed to her sister into a gnarled tree that grows out of lava rock, so he would forever be in her bosom.

Lehua, seeing that her husband did not return that day, went searching for her love. She was broken to find that he had been turned into a twisted tree that stood fixed in the lava rock. She cried for four days, praying to the gods Kane and Lono for her husband to be returned to her in his human form. For days nothing happened, and then her prayers were answered in a dream when she was told that she could be reunited with Ohi`a. Lehua would have to sacrifice her human form and turn into a flower that bloomed on the tree her husband had been changed to out of spite.

Without hesitation, Lehua agreed to be reunited with Ohi`a and she was transformed into the red and orange blossom that blooms on the Ohi`a lehua tree twice a year.

The legend told that if the flower was picked from the tree, rain would fall from the sky in Hawai`i on a clear day. These were the tears of Lehua being separated from her husband again.

Ben remembered this legend he had grown up with as a light mist descended upon the island. He and Kalima neared Pu'uwai and could see the people gathered outside of where his wife was being held. The fact there were others gave Ben strength as he approached the crowd of villagers who had the look of pilikia on their faces.

Yoshio and Shige emerged from the house they were holding Ella in. Ella came out of the house last with a look of dread, knowing that they would not find Harold. She knew her husband had reached the inevitable conclusion there must be a reckoning between what had happened and what was going to happen. She looked around at the ground, searching for something. All she saw were lava rocks of significant size used for the garden of the house, which had a rock wall, serving as a gate. The villagers who had not fled gathered outside the rock wall when they saw the two armed agitators take Emma in. They gathered there out of concern for her and themselves, hoping sheer number would deter anything bad from happening to Ella.

When Shige saw Ben and Kalima walking towards them without the papers and Harold, he turned to Yoshio.

"Why are they returning without what we have asked them, Yoshio?" he said in anger. "We have told them that we will kill the woman if they returned to us empty-handed as they have. We have no choice but to show them that we are not playing games here. We mean what we say. Get the woman and let us show them what happens when they try to play games like children."

"Please, Shige. Let me talk with them and see what has happened here," Yoshio said to Shige.

Yoshio turned his attention from Shige and gazed at Ella. He knew that she must die if he did not find where the papers were. There was no other choice.

"Where are the papers, Ben?" Yoshio asked Kanehale. "The pilot has said he intends to kill your wife now if you do not return with the things that have been taken from him. And yet here you are, returning with nothing. What are we to do?"

"Harold has left, just like the others, Yoshio," Ben said to him. "He left several hours ago on a raft back to Kaua'i. I assume he has taken the papers with him. You could not find them in his house. I cannot get the papers Yoshio and this is our home. Not his. We have done what you have asked, let Ella be."

"Ben, he will kill her now," Yoshio said.

"Take the gun from him, Yoshio," Ben said. "You have lived with us as if you are a brother and you are our brother. We need you now. Take the gun, I beg you."

Shige knew enough to know that they had not done what he asked of them. He reached for the pistol from his boot.

Ben, seeing the pilot reach for his gun, shouted with all the air in his lungs.

"Maka koa," he yelled as Shige pointed at the charging seven-foot-tall man, firing a single shot ringing out, followed by two more.

Unphazed, Ben Kanehale grabbed Shige and lifted him above his head, hurling him with all the might he had within his wounded body. Ben Kanehale fell to the ground while the pilot sailed through the air, crashing into the stone wall. Ben went forward still, slashing the throat of Shige like he had done so many times hunting for pig.

Ella lifted the smallest of the lava rocks from the garden and charged forward to the pilot, who was attempting to hold his spilling blood in. She fell on him with the rock as hard as she could on the head, splitting his skull in a ferocious upheaval like an exploded watermelon.

Shige's lifeless body fell to the ground in an unceremonious thud as Ella went to her husband. He was bleeding from the gunshot wounds that had seared through his body. One on the leg, one in the groin, and one in the shoulder.

"Are you ok, Ella?" he asked, not thinking of his own poor state.

Bloodstained Ella's dress as she contemplated how to stop the bleeding. She looked at Yoshio, who held the shotgun in his hands as if it were a curse.

The villagers looked at the man who they had taken in once. He fumbled with words and knew he would either have to kill them or himself. There was no way out of it now as the body of Shige lay bleeding and unrecognizable.

"A'ole," they shouted as the villagers began to circle around Yoshio, who was trembling like an animal caught in a trap. "Lolo."

"I am sorry that I made the choice I did, but I had to out of love for the nation that my family is from," he said, fleeing from the villagers.

Yoshio went to his wife Irene. It was the last time the two would ever speak to each other.

"What I did, I did it for us," Yoshio said to his wife and love of his life. "I thought that if the Japanese were coming, there was no way to save our family if we did not help the pilot."

"What happened to the pilot?" Irene asked. She had not seen or heard anything that had taken place in the village outside of her own home.

His silence left her, the same as he did not long after, leaving her with the life that was to remain after he was gone forever. She thought about the first time they met in Japan and the life he had promised her.

She thought about their wedding day and how his mother gave her a necklace left to her by her departed mother. She remembered how he had promised her a life that she would always cherish. The thought of the day they decided to come to Hawai'i came to her and she cursed it. That was the last time she thought about what Yoshio had promised her, as she prepared for what she must do now.

Yoshio, shamed by the thought of failing the person he loved most in the world, gave up the thought of staying alive.

He knew when he helped the pilot he would have to turn on the people he loved in the name of where he came from and where he was born. The decision to help his countryman in death by honor was innate. The decision had already been made before it was asked of him. His destiny and that of the pilot were intertwined, woven on the island of Ni'ihau as two sons of Japan who made it there by the hand of destiny.

It was clear to him what he had to do then as he went to the place there that had made him happy many times. He went down from the village, not far. It was where he would go when he missed home and got scared of the future for he and his wife who had stood by him, even when times got tough. She didn't have to stay by his side, even when he told her that they must move to Ni'ihau from Kaua'i where he was born. Irene was born in Japan, and with Yoshio having been born on Kaua'i and a second-generation Japanese immigrant, he had promised her the world. Irene loved America but did not like Niʻihau. She loved Kauaʻi and often told Yoshio that she would prefer to live there.

He wished he had listened to her at that moment as he listened to the silence abound. He thought of the Waimea Canyon, near where he was born on Kauaʻi. He looked to his parents' homeland, Japan. He wished he had never been poisoned by the American dream. He wanted so badly to have stayed at home and gone off to war like the rest of his peers who would now carry on the fight he felt so connected to, but would never be a part of outside of Niʻihau.

The birds chirped their prayer to nature, feeling the end of the day. They were unbothered by the troubles of man and stayed swayed only by the rhythm of nature. Their long never-ending song gave Yoshio the courage to end his sound.

He pointed the gun at himself, saying goodbye to the world he had known and the love that he had. The birds flew away, troubled by the sound that resembled nothing they had heard before. Silence followed as the waves crashed on the shores, as they had always done before.

Journey to Kauai

Howard Kaleohana looked at the Garden Isle streched out before the men who rowed in unison towards their goal, tired but still holding on.

"That's it men, we're more than halfway there," he told them, the same thing he had been telling them beyond the halfway mark. "With every row, we are that much closer to putting this whole thing behind us."

Many of them wondered what the world had become since they had been away. For most of the six, it had been some time since they last left the island. They had grown used to the solitude that they had come to know and call their daily life on Ni'ihau. Many of them had not been back to Kaua'i, or civilization in quite some time. The events had turned their daily lives upisde down, to the point they were rowing away from the homes they had created to flee from the foreign threat that had come to their island uninvited.

The island of Kaua'i is the oldest of the Hawaiian islands, created out of the bosom of the earth by a large shield valcano that began erupting 10 million years ago. The eruption formed the modern day peaks of Mount Waialeale and Kawakini that tower over the basin that is the extinct volcano crater. The two peaks are all that remain of the once powerful volcano that created the island. After millions of years of erosion, the two peaks stand in eroding defiance of time and the elements that have slowy desinigrated its very being.

The Weeping Wall forms the back of the crater, where all the rivers on Kaua'i start after collecting water like a giant vase that now flow through the old lava tubes that once formed the island, serving as the heart of the old and current island.

Both Ni'ihau and Kaua'i were formed by shield volcanos forming the two islands seperated by 17-miles at their closest points. Over millions of years, the two islands formed when a shift in the Pacific Plate allowed magma to flow to the surface. Ni'ihau began forming around 5 million years ago when a shield valcano off of Kaua'i's eruption began to break the surface of the vast Pacific Ocean, forming Lehua Rock of basalt in an underwater explosion, and Ni'ihau.

The first people reached the sacred sands on Kaua'i an estimated 1,800 years ago. It's said to be the first island the Polynesians inhabited in the archipeligo. Their ships reached the western shores of Kaua'i, where there are heiaus that remain today, rumored to have been used for human sacrifice.

Captain Cook "discovered" the Hawaiian

archipeligo for Europe when he made landfall on January, 20th, 1778, in what is now Waimea town on the west coast of Kaua'i. Cook landed on the sacred shores after spotting Oahu in the early evening of January 19th. Prevailing winds carried the two ships to the nearby island of Kaua'i which lies 73 miles to the west from the island of Oahu.

In search of freshwater, Cook anchored his 105 foot HMS Endeavor, and 108 foot HMS Resolution some two miles off the coast of modern day Waimea town after first encountering Hawaiians off the south shore of Kaua'i, trading iron and scarp metal with them for fish and Uala (sweet potatoes). The uala were a staple to the Hawaiian culture for centuries and had been brought to the islands by the Polynesians who had acquired it from South America. The uala from Ni'ihau were legendary in size and sweetness.

Cook and his crew were searching for the Northwest Passage and fresh water, which made the Waimea River an appealing landing spot. Some Hawaiians were allowed to come aboard before Cook and his men touched ground near the Waimea River. They were greated by several hundred Hawaiians who gave them pigs and bananas when they stepped foot on the sands of Kaua'i for the first time.

Now 163 years later, Howard and his men rowed towards Waimea, desperate for safe passage and water. With Niʻihau at their backs, the Waimea Pier came into view.

"That's it, we're right there," he said to the others while he rowed with them. "Just like that. When we get to the pier, let me do the speaking if there are any guards."

As they came closer, they could see there were several armed guards patrolling the pier. The guards noticed the dingy and started shouting at the men, who could barely make out what they were saying at first, but could hear them as they got closer.

"Where are you coming from and who are you," they asked in one iteration or another. The exhausted men heaved with all their remaining strength to get to land, as some were at the point of fainting from exhaustion.

As they dingy pulled up to the pier on the calm morning of December 12, the exhausted men gave their final strength on the last pulls.

"This here is a Robinson boat," Howard said to the armed guards, who took this as enough of a confirmation they were not enemy soldiers. The island of Kauaʻi and the territory of Hawaiʻi was now under martial law.

Alymer Robinson was summoned at once and he showed up to the pier, shocked and amazed at the men who had given there all to make it to Waimea in such a fashion. He had never heard of men doing the channel crossing in a dingy, let alone with the military under such high alert looking for enemy ships.

"Howard, what has happened that caused you to row your way to Kaua'i and Waimea?" Alymer asked his worker, who looked him back in the eyes with a somber darkness.

"We have much to tell you boss," Howard said, looking at the men who rowed with him from Ni'ihaua. "These men have done all they could to get us here and they are weak. They need food and water, then some rest, boss."

"They will have all three without delay," Alymer said, ushering the men into the back of his truck. He drove them to a nearby Chinese restaurant and fed them and listened to Howard's version of events that had transpired since December 7th - 13th.

Howard, not knowing what had happened since they had departed the island, assumed that it was still being held by gunpoint and that the Kanehales and all the other villagers were still at the mercy of the pilot and Yoshio Harada.

Upon hearing the story, Alymer went to the phone and called naval captain Jack Mizuha and informed him of what he had been told by Howard Kaleohano. He let him know in detail of the Japanese pilot terrorizing the local population on his land and the need for their armed support in removing the threat and restoring liberty to the island of Ni'ihau.

A squad of 12 men were assembled at once

on Kaua'i to go to Ni'ihau and observe the situation. Alymer joined them, leaving the shores of Kaua'i and Waimea town on a lighthouse tender in the early afternoon of December 13.

They arrived at the sands of Ni'ihau in the early morning hours of December 14th, guided by the setting sun and their mission. They did not know what to expect. Some of them anticipated the first hand to hand combat in the fresh war, with the United States now at war with Japan, Germany, and Italy. These men knew they would see service in this fresh war, but few anticipated it would be so soon.

Howard and the men stayed in Waimea only long enough to get water and food, going with the 14 military men and Alymer back to Ni'ihau and their homes. For Howard, the only thing left for him was the papers he had held close since obtaining them after the pilot had landed. He knew that it was his purpose all along to hold onto those papers and turn them over to Alymer and the military. It was the right hting to do in his mind, and it felt good when he handed the papers over to Alymer, who studied them briefly.

"Simply amazing," he said, looking over the battle plans and maps of Pearl Harbor. "This is truly something, Howard. We are thankful that you have kept this and given it to us."

Alymer handed the documents over to the comander of the 299th Infantry Regiment expedition, Captain Jack Mizuha, who thanked him for the documents. Howard watched and felt proud of what he had done, even if it had cost him his house

Their hearts raced, and their minds wandered in flushed exuberance, brought on with each passing jolt on the boat brought on by a passing wave.

Alymer Robinson reflected on all the conversations he had with Yoshio and Irene. He thought about what it would take for them to turn on all the villagers. He knew that it would be difficult whatever was to happen when he got to Ni`ihau, but he was the steward of this island. It was his birthright. He felt partially responsible for this situation as his kinship with the island was almost inseperable from how he felt about himself. Every person who was on that island was given permission by himself. Anything that happened there, he was in the know about. There was not a movement on the island that didn't happen without his say so, and he took pride in that fact. Ni`ihau was like a child to Alymer, the child he never had. Alymer wasn't interested in anything in life other than his education, which he had received at Harvard, and the island.

He cared about his family, but Alymer didn't want to participate in the shameful act as he saw it, of incest. It was enough for Alymer to have control of the island. The villagers and people of Ni'ihau were his children and he saw them as inncoent as simple children and did everything he could to protect them from the harsh outside world.

Alymer even took care of the animals on the island and had gone as far as to nurse White Hawaiian Monk Seals that had been injured by sharks back to health. He had a deep love for the land and the aina. This uninvited guest that had come to the island stood for everything that Alymer and his family had tried to keep away. He and his family had run that island without interferance since they had first acquired it in 1864

They stepped ashore at Keei where the men had launched from a few nights before, hidden by the moonlight and still compelled forward by what had brought them to the island. Their rifles pointed up the entire time, searching for the possible enemy that could lurk at every corner and behind every rock. The smell of smoke and burning oil filled their noses as they inched closer to where it came from.

The first people they encountered told of Ben's injuries and said the threat of the Japanese pilot was no more.

"What do you mean the pilot is no more?" Alymer asked.

"The pilot has gone and it was the woman Kanehale that done it for she moved quick with the rock and ended his occupation," a man told

Alymer and the other men.

They were lead to where Ben and his wife were as the villagers were doing what they could to tend to the wounds that Ben had sustained. The navy men quickly located Ishimatsu and Irene Hamada, who were summoned before Alymer, the Kanehales, and the rest gathered.

"What has happened here should have never happened," Alymer said to the Kanehales. "I am sorry that I could not come here and relieve you of the demon that came. I would have shot him myself had I been allowed to sail across the channel, but the navy forbode me from doing just that. I would have loved to catch him in the act."

Ben was shot three times, but his bleeding had been stopped. He watched as Irene Hamada and Ishimatsu Shintani were brought ushered in before Alymer and the Navy.

"You had to of known what they were going to do, Irene," they said to her, as she remained steadfast. "Irene, they are going to put you in a place that you don't want to go to if you don't cooperate with us."

No matter the threats that we put in her way, Irene Harada did not crack. She was arrested, along with Ishimatsu.

"Why did you try to bribe Harold into giving you the papers of the pilot?" they asked the old beekeeper who was born in Japan and was a first generation immigrant to America.

"I did not want Harold, or the pilot to do anything foolish that they might regret," he told them. "And it looks like my worst fears came true."

The pair of prisoners were taken back to Kauai, along with Ben Kanehale, who received treatment for his gunshot wounds that he survived and overcame. He was later awarded the Purple Heart in Honolulu on August 15, 1945. Kanehale was also honored with the Medal of Merit on May 10, 1946.

His wife, Ella, was awarded nothing but the survival of her and her husband. That was enough for her, for she knew how close they came to a different outcome. She accompanied her husband to the ceremonies and smiled the entire time. She was proud of what they had done and she did what she had to do to survive. They all did. It was basic human instinct. She didn't need a medal or recognition to know who the heroes were that day. There were plenty.

The ones who lost their lives, were the ones who had made the most basic mistake in their actions. they had failed to hold that basic principle so dear to the Hawaiian culture, which is aloha.

If only their actions had been guided by the principles of aloha, perhaps they would all still be alive.

Ben Kanehale and Ella returned to Niʻihau after he had healed from his wounds. They lived the same way they had before the pilot had come to Ni'ihau and they continued living this way until their time on the island came to an end. Ben passed away on Kaua'i in 1962 at the age of 71. He was buried in Pu'uwai on Ni'ihau. Ella followed him in death in 1974 at the age of 66. She was buried in Pu'uwai, the same place she was born in.

Ella retrieved the pistol after Ben was shot in 1941, but lost it in the process of helping him. It was never found. The Shotgun that Yoshio used to take his life, washed up from a flood against a wall some years later. One of the machine guns was also never recovered.

Harold received the Medal of Freedom in 1946 and was given $800 by the federal government to rebuild his house that had been burned down by Shige and Yoshio in their search for the papers.

Irene Harada and Ishimatsu were jailed at first on Kaua'i at the Waimea jail in the same cell, then later on Kaua'i in the Wailua River jail. They were the first Japanese Americans to be detained following the attack on Pearl Harbor. They were the first of 120,000 Japanese that would follow in their footsteps through internment.

Ishimatsu kept telling Irene, "It was your husband's actions that have got us in here. If he cared more for you, he would have kept to the middle way and not got involved in that pilot's business."

With the loss of her husband still fresh, Irene endured Ishimatsu and his insults to a dead man. He kept repeating the same iteration of blame for their prediciment, and Irene stopped eating for five days. She went on a hunger strike to get the old man to stop, and it nearly killed her.

Ishimatsu was eventually moved to the mainland for interment, and he later returned to Ni'ihau after he was released from interment after the war. Ishimatsu became and American citizen in 1960.

Irene Harada maintained her innocence the entire time of her 31-month internment and was never officially charged with treason, although accused and questioned in handcuffs by an FBI investigator. She was jailed at the Wailua Jail for three months before she was moved to Oahu where she stayed for over two years. Her youngest daughter was given to the care of her older sister on Kaua'i while she was in jail.

Harada served most of her prison sentence on Sand Island in Oahu, and Honolulu prison camps. Harada and five other women were the only women prisoners at the interment camps during the duration of the war. Harada was ordered to interment "for her own good."

Irene was paroled on June 29, 1944. She returned home to Kaua'i from Oahu upon her release. Her three daughters and sister were waiting for her when she arrived home at last where she was born. Irene lived on Kauaʻi in relative peace and aloha for the rest of her life, though she often looked back at the time in her life that caused her so much pain and anguish.

In a Japanese television interview in 1992, Irene Harada admitted she had felt sorry for the pilot and wanted to help him.

When she was incarcerated, Irene would often think about what she could have done differently to avoid the tragedy that took place and took the life of the person she loved the most in the world. She would think it over and over, wondering what would have happened if she had told them not to do anything and to let it all pass over.

The number of detainees grew over the course of her interment and she would confide in the other prisoners, but was always careful and never allowed her grief much air to breathe. She did take comfort in the fact she could be around others who had lost their daily lives to be imprisoned, and they would make small gift to each other and write letters. It gave her some solace to have something, even if she had lost so much. It was easy for the other prisoners to see the sadness that was endured by all, and in particular the tall and stern Harada.

Irene often wondered if her husband would have listened to what she had told them what was going to happen with their failed plot.

She wondered about every detail imaginable, and then she would think it over some more.

Irene opened a sewing store school in Kapaa town on Kaua'i, opening it on a second floor above a popular jewelery store. Her brother operated the jewelery store and as the days went by, the memory of what had happened became less fresh in her mind.

The memories would stir up again on occassion. There would be visitors from Japan from time to time. They were looking to make things right in their own minds, or come to terms what they had done in their old age. One of these visitors was Japanese Navy Captain Fuchida Mitsuo, who stopped by on July 20, 1953, while traveling to Hawaii on a Christian mission.

He had found religion after the war and learned of the Ni'ihau Incident in an anonymous letter. He hurried to meet Irene on Kaua'i, and when he did, he apologized to her for what she had been through from the heart.

"I do not blame him for what he did because he had Japanese blood flowing in him," she told the ex-captain. "It was not wrong of him because of the blood flowing in him. He was born in America and was an American, so they are not wrong in saying that we committed treason, but he was not wrong because of his blood."

"That is a beautiful sentiment," he told her in response."

In September of 1955, Irene was visited by a newspaper reporter from Japan, who asked her if she would like to go to Japan to visit her late husband's parents, her brother, and the family of Shige.

"I wish I could do that, but I must work for the sake of my children," she told him. "I've thought about family suicide many times, but changed my mind and have worked day and night"

Irene promised Yoshio that she would send their three children to college, and she held true to that promise.

The same reporter returned one day with a roundtrip ticket to Japan. The offer was tempting, but she refused it and said, "if I took the ticket, it would only lead to confusion and bring up old feeling about the war and the past that would be misunderstood. It would cause hardship for my children here, and for that reason I cannot go. I apologize that I cannot accept your most genorous offer."

Shige and Yoshio's remains were sought out by Yoshio's younger brother, who had been discharged from military service in 1946. The younger brother went to Ni'ihau to retireve the remains and was unable to retrieve the remains of the pilot as they were under the control of the immigration center on Kaua'i, where they were then transfered to the naval base, then the Yokohama columbarium. On the 15th year after the incident, Shige's family collected his remains at the Ehime Prefecture. His family returned his remains to Japan.

The returning of his remains sparked national Japanese interest in the 1970s which reulted in even more people seeking out Irene Harada on Kaua'i for accounts of what had happened.

Irene one day decided that everything had to happen the way it did and that she had tried to tell them what she thought at the time. She knew that she had played a part in the tragedy. It was something that she thought about for the rest of her life. Most of all she thought about what life would be like if she still had her husband there to help her through it. That is what she missed the most. All the other things were just details, but her husband was the thing that she had lived for and she knew in order to survive, she would have to find that love in a different place.

She would look to Ni'ihau often from Waimea later on in life. She had liked the time she spent there, but she had alway dreaded living there, from the moment Yoshio had told her they would move from Kaua'i. The media was a constant reminder of what had happened in those guilded days back in her youth, and as the world changed, she would look to Ni'ihau to think of the time that had passed and all the things that had changed in the world and in herself.

In the fall of 1992, Irene visited Japan on a pilgramage. She visited her parents' familiar homes, and the went to the pilot's family home in Ehime Japan. At the age of 79, Irene Harada accomplished the Shikoku pilgrimage, something she had told herself she would do as a 22-year-old girl so many decades before.

Irene Harada passed away on October 1, 1996, at the age of 81. Her last thoughts were on that of her husband and their three children. She was happy to be on her way to see him again. She focused on the sound of the birds outside her window as everything else in her world faded away, and then there was silence again after a life of noise.

There is a monument to Shigenori Nishikaichi that stands 12-feet tall in Hashihama, Imabari, Ehime Prefecture. Japan erected the monument before it was known what had happened to Shige, and it was believed that he died on December 7, 1941, in the attack on Pearl Harbor. It was not know what became of Shige until his family reclaimed his remains in 1956.

Engraved on the monument are the words, "Having expended every effort, he achieved the greatest honor of all by dying a soldier's death in battle, destroying both himself and his beloved plane... His meritorious deed will live forever."

Ni'ihau leans firmly back

Long before 1864 when the then Sinclair family acquired Ni'ihau fee simple for $10,000, the island was ruled by chiefs or Alii who governed by the kapu system. This system governed life for the citizens of the island even before the Kingdom of Hawai'i and eventually the Robinson family.

"Ni'ihau i ke kiku," or Ni'ihau leans firmly back in English, and has always been a traditional Hawaiian chant. It gives rise to the name "The Forbidden Island" long before the Robinson family came to make the island their home. The island was always standing firmly back from the rest of the archipelago, ever since the days of creation. The Hawaiian myths sing of this basic truth of Ni'ihau.

Ni'ihau and Kaua'i were the last of the islands of the archipelago to come under the control of the Kingdom of Hawai'i and Kamehameha the Great. While most of the islands fell to Kamehameha by 1795, Ni'ihau and Kaua'i remained free and independent of his control. Ni'ihau and Kaua'i were ruled independently by King Kaumualii. He was the last king to rule Kaua'i and Ni'ihau independent of the Hawaiian

Kingdom and the Kamehamehas.

It had long been believed in Hawaiian tradition that Ni'ihau was the first home of Pele and was in existence by the time her canoe reached the golden sands of Ni'ihau. She would have arrived on Ni'ihau before the story of Ohi'a and Lehua. Pele did not reside long in Ni'ihau before eventually moving to Kaua'i and down the chain of islands, settling on Hawai'i island where there are five active volcanos to this day. But a common theme arises in Hawaiian mythology and that is that Ni'ihau was Pele's first home in Hawai'i.

Ni'ihau, based on science, was thought to have formed approximately 4.8 million years ago. This formation was based on the nearby island of Kaua'i, which Ni'ihau is dependent on the rain shadow that brings a small amount of moisture to the island every year.

The first great chief of Ni'ihau that is left to us in history is of Kahelelani, whose name carries on today in association with the colorful shells that make up the Ni'ihau lei. The shells are often called Kahelelani shells, and the island itself was at one time referred to as Ni'ihau a Kahelelani, carrying with it the name of the great ali'i through the ages.

Another great ali'i to rule Ni'ihau was Ka'eo, who defeated a warrior chief in Kawaihoa to gain complete control of Ni'ihau. Instead of killing Kawaihoa, Ka'eo banished the warrior chief to the southernmost point of Niʻihau, which is often confused as being another island as it sticks out after relative flatness giving the appearance of another island from afar. The southern point of Niʻihau is now named after the banished warrior Kawaihoa.

Kamakahelei of Kauaʻi would later serve as the chiefess aliʻi of Niʻhau and Kauaʻi and would give birth to the last independent king of Niʻhau and Kauaʻi in Kaumualiʻi. Kaumualiʻi served as king of both Niʻhau and Kauaʻi from 1796 until 1810 when both islands eventually joined the Kingdom of Hawaiʻi in 1810 without bloodshed.

From 1810 until 1865 when the Robinson family leagally acquired the island of Niihau, its people flourished while standing firmly back from the rest of the kingdom and even the near-by island of Kauai.

Before the time of Kaumualiʻi, a legend was told about five fisherman who journeyed from Kauaʻi to the shores of Niʻihau.

Ekahi, Elua, Ekolu, Eha, and Elima lived in the days when man-eating spirits feasted on men. These five men made their way to Niʻihau to fish and on the first day they fished, their catch was plentiful and abundant.

After the successful fishing trip, the five men lay out on the golden sands of Niʻihau and cooked their catch. They fell asleep on the sands of the beach with their bellies full and their needs satisfied. The stars strung out across the black sail of a sky and the five men rested their minds and bodies.

When the sun broke the darkness of the night, the five men were now four. They looked around and noticed that Elima had vanished.

One man said, "This is an evil place. The spirits have eaten Elima and we must leave before they consume us."

The leader of the group, Ekahi said, "He has probably left us to go find more fish and places to fish. We will wait for him. You will see, he will return to us before long."

The men waited the day, hoping Elima would return to them safe and sound. As the day passed and night settled down on them again, they began to grow fearful. They fell asleep despite their fears.

When they awoke in the morning, Eha was missing from them. With only three of them left now, Ekolu pronounced the island as "an evil place."

Ekahi agreed that it was an evil place that they must leave, but he believed they were fisherman and bound to do what must be done.

"We must kill these evil things," he said, deciding that they all must sleep together.

When they awoke the next morning to the sounds of Ekolu being pulled by a flying man-eating monster, they were frozen in fear when they saw him consumed entirely.

With two of them left, they devised a plan

to kill the man-eating monsters so nobody had to live in fear ever again of the monsters as they had these last three days.

Ekahi had a plan to lure the man-eating monsters into a log house they built. Inside the log house, there were two wooden images that were made to look like men. They were completed with two mussel shells each for eyes, and the men now waited for the evil spirits to return as they hid near the log house.

The two evil spirits returned and saw the newly constructed houses with the two wooden images that looked like men within. The spirits waited for the men to go to sleep, but saw that their eyes did not close. After waiting for a long part of the night, the spirits grew tired of waiting and went inside the log house to eat the men. The spirits soon found the men were stringy like wood as they toiled to consume them. Elua sprung out of his hiding spot and threw a torch on the log house, igniting it in a fireball that consumed the evil spirits.

With the evil spirits now killed on the island of Ni'ihau, fisherman were now free to fish there from Kaua'i in the days long before the Robinsons called the island their home.

Robinson Island

Niʻihau, as it was long before man, was an isolated island that formed in the shadow of Kauaʻi. To this day it relies on the nearby island of Kauaʻi for both sustenance and sanctuary, but is steadfast in its solitude and forbidden status. Despite the fact that it is Hawaiʻi state law all beach is public access, the island of Niʻihau is an exception to the rule.

Visitors to the island are on an invitation basis only, and at one time, the island was available for a safari hunting tour that ended in 2020 during the pandemic. It has not restarted since and remains to this day off limits to uninvited guests, in part because of what transpired with the Niʻihau Incident, but events that transpired after it in the 1950s and beyond.

The island is now run by two brothers named Keith and Bruce who are the foreman of the island. They are Alymer's nephews on account of their uncle never having children of his own. The two brothers reside on Kauaʻi and still visit the island of Niʻihau at least once a week, usually in their blue helicopter that was used in the movie Jurassic Park. Keith can be seen driving around Waimea town in his Jeep Scambler, always wearing his green hardhat.

News spread of the Niʻihau Incident throughout the country like wildfire as the war raged on for four years and it was one the first and finest stories of bravery and of the sacrifice that was to come on both sides.

For the United States, the Niʻihau Incident and the aftermath have been linked to the interment of 120,000 Japanese and Japanese Americans that were to be held prisoner throughout the course of the war. The loyalty of the Haradas to their homeland served as a stark reminder of what could occur nationally, and the incident fueled the interment that stands as the lone act of its kind in American history.

Alymer continued to serve as the foreman of the island until he passed away in 1967. Alymer, having no sons or daughters of his own, spent most of his time working. This left him with little time to cultivate a family of his own. The island was passed to his brother Lester in 1967, but ownership was short-lived as Lester passed away in 1969. Lester's sons Bruce and Keith took over ownership of the island and managed it in the same fashion as was taught to them by their uncle Alymer.

The island became the possession of the Robinson family when they purchased it outright from King Kamehameha V for a fee simple $10,000 in gold bars and a baby grand piano, which was thrown in as the kicker to sweeten the pot. The deal was struck between the to-be Robinson family and the Kingdom of Hawaiʻi and two different kings in 1864-1865 with several conditions imposed.

Elizabeth Sinclair arrived on Ni'ihau via New Zealand, which she came to as a foreigner from Scotland in 1841. Sinclair's husband and oldest son died at sea in 1846, leaving her widowed and sole executive of their estate. She and the extended family prospered in New Zealand as cattle ranchers, but Elizabeth was never able to come to terms with the feeling of emptiness and loss that had filled her since the loss of the two most important people in her world.

Sinclair longed for death, or a new life and eventually came to the decision to set sail from New Zealand in 1863 in search of a life outside of what she and her family had known for so many years. The family had made the decision to leave the year prior, so had plenty of time to gather resources like a baby grand piano to load onto their three mast barque named "Bessie" prior to departure from New Zealand.

In search of paradise and a new home, the 12 family members with the names Sinclair, Gay, and Robinson visited Tahiti, followed by British Columbia. They then turned west to Hawai'i, not contented with life in the first places they visited. The family found the Hawaiian Kingdom and their king when they made harbor with their ship, family, and crew.

In search of a new home, several lands were offered to the family including what is now Ford Island on Oahu, Kahuku, and a tract of land that stood between Diamond Head and the city of Honolulu.

None of these lands caught the fancy of Sinclair, but she did like the archipelago and decided to wait until the right property was offered to the family. And that tactic proved to be fruitful as the island of Ni`ihau was eventually listed for sale by the Kingdom of Hawai`i and two of Sinclair's sons sailed to Ni`ihau from Oahu to see exactly what the island was like. They found the island to be extremely lush and vibrant on account of the abundance of rain that had fallen on the island that particular year.

Wanting to raise cattle on the island, the brothers found the conditions to be just perfect for their desires. The lush tropical foliage was thriving in the volcanic soil that year, growing most unusually thick and lush due to the abnormally heavy rainfall. Francis and James Sinclair sailed back to Oahu with the good news, telling their mother all about the tropical island paradise of Ni`ihau. They were enchanted with the idea of owning their own island. The thought of such a thing was magnificent and gave them hope for a new home all to themselves.

They worked on their mother and prodded her, in hopes to convince her to purchase the island. After much convincing, they were able to persuade their mother to purchase the island of Ni`ihau with the intention of turning it into a functioning cattle ranch.

After much consideration, a price was agreed upon with the Minister of Foreign Affairs for the Kingdom of Hawai`i.

The people of Niʻihau were not in favor of the sale and appealed the ordeal to the Minister of the Interior. The appeal was cast away in favor of the sale by the Kingdom and on January 20th, 1864, Elizabeth Sinclair purchased Niʻihau fee simple from Kamehameha V in the names of her two sons Francis, and James.

The deal was agreed to in November of 1863 with King Kamehameha IV, but upon his death from chronic asthma on November 30, 1863, the deal was carried over and finished with his brother King Kamehameha V the following year on the 86th anniversary of Captain James Cook's arrival on Kauaʻi and first landing in the Hawaiian archipelago.

The New York Times reported that while signing the deed of sale of the island, King Kamehameha was quoted as saying, "Niʻihau is yours. But the day may come when Hawaiians are not as strong in Hawaiʻi as they are now. When that day comes, please do what you can to help them."

Royal Patent No. 2944 described the sale as 61,038 acres. The acreage on the patent was not correct but was an estimation at the time. The island is just under 70 square miles and has a peak elevation of 1,281 feet.

The patent gave the Sinclair family all the parcels on the island of Niʻihau except for two tracts of land. One of the tracts was around 50 acres and was sold to a man named Papapa, who later sold the acreage to the Sinclairs/Robinsons for an unremarkable price. The other tract was granted to Koakanu the Great Mahele in 1848.

The Koakanu tract was eventually sold to the Sinclair family for around $1,000. This came after Koakanu's wife convinced him to sell the property for the sum after he had apparently refused anyone to cross his property, even going as far as to forbid any boats from making it within a half mile of the shoreline of his property.

With the sale of the last tract on Ni`ihau sold to the Robinsons, all of the island was secured and outright owned by the family in 1865, one year after their initial purchase.

The Robinsons took to forming a ranch on the island in the old tradition of rent paid for one or two days of work. The family had brought with them one cow, and sheep from New Zealand, but went to purchasing fine sheep from all around Hawaii, bringing them to the island.

They employed the remaining Hawaiian population on the island which was estimated to be around 500 when they purchased the island in 1864, and later around 250 in 1865 when they owned the entirety of the island.

There was some hardship in the sale of the island to the family of Scots as many of the Hawaiians had not legally filed their rightful claims for Kuleana lands in the Great Mahele of 1864. This resulted in some of the longtime residents of the island leaving the island for good, making way for the Robinsons' new home for the 13 family members that all now primarily called the island home.

In the years that followed, the family made the island their home and tried to make it as hospitable as possible. They soon found that the lush island they had first sailed to was but a fluke rainy year, making the island appear as something other than a burning desert in the middle of the Pacific Ocean. On most years, the island did not receive enough rain (the island averages 30-40 inches of rain a year) to be a consistent producing ranch for agriculture.

This did not dissuade the Sinclair family from trying and as the years passed, Eliza was considered as a chiefess amongst the Hawaiians on Ni'ihau and Kaua'i. Finding life much more hospitable on the island of Kaua'i, the Sinclair/Robinson family increased their holdings in land on the Hawaiian archipelago by purchasing 21,844 acres on nearby Kaua'i in Makaweli for $15,000. They purchased this land on Kaua'i one year after the Ni'ihau purchase, securing the Sinclair/Robinson family as one of the largest landowners in the Hawaiian Kingdom.

Elizabeth Sinclair lived out the rest of her days on her residence in Pakala Village on Kaua'i, occasionally venturing over to Ni'ihau to visit where her son Francis Sinclair Jr. took over as the island manager starting in 1864 after the purchase. Francis was the sole manager of the island for nearly 20 years, making sure all operations on the ranch went as smoothly as possible for the family. Francis made his home on the western shore of the island in Kiekie. He later made his home in the higher elevation of Makaweli near the Pakala Village on Kaua'i.

Francis left the islands for a brief time to travel to New Zealand where he was married to his cousin, Isabella McHutcheson, on August 7, 1866.

Francis became the sole owner of Ni'ihau when his brother James Sinclair passed away in 1873 from injuries he succumbed to after sustaining them in New Zealand. The deed to Ni'ihau had been signed in Francis and James' names when the purchase was completed, leaving only Francis as a remaining owner.

A year later in 1874, Francis became a citizen of the Kingdom of Hawaii. For the next decade, Francis managed Ni'ihau and the residents of the island as a citizen of the kingdom. In 1883, Francis made the decision to leave Hawai'i and the kingdom to make his life elsewhere in the world. He left management of the island of Ni'ihau to his two nephews - Aubrey Robinson, and Francis Gay.

In 1884, a year after leaving the island, Francis' wife Isabella published the only book on native Hawaiian plants in color at the time. It was titled 'Indigenous Flowers of the Hawaiian Islands' and brought some literary success to the family, displaying their knowledge of the islands for all the world to see.

Isabella gathered information on the plants in several locations on Kaua'i and Ni'ihau with the help of Hawaiians who aided her in understanding the different species. Her love for the people and plants poured out into the book and she would paint the pictures with her own hand, gatherings as much information as possible on the plants via the Hawaiians, who would pour all their worldly knowledge of their plants in Waimea Canyon and on Niʻihau into the young woman who showed such passion and love for the plants and people of the the two islands. The book served as an important historical marker of many of the native plant species that later became extinct or threatened in many cases.

The book consisted of 44 pages of color illustrations and its dedication reads, "To the Hawaiian Chiefs and People who have been most appreciative friends, and most lenient critics, this work is affectionately inscribed."

Isabella is one of the first documented individuals to express concern over the encroachment of invasive species on native Hawaiian plants, a common theme the islands contend with to this day that has been exasperated by an ever-changing environment under constant bombardment from new species being introduced, sometimes unintentionally. One shining modern example of this is the accidental introduction of the coqui frog to Maui, and the Big Island via a shipping container of Walmart plants inbound from the mainland in the early 1980's.

In 1891, Francis Sinclair Jr. sold all of his interest in Niʻihau to his sisters - Jane Gray, Helen Robinson, and Audrey Robinson. A year later on October 16, 1892, Elizabeth Sinclair passed away on the family's estate in Makaweli. Francis and Isabella moved to California after selling their Hawaii interests and stayed there until Isabella passed away in San Jose on December 29, 1900. Francis then moved to England and pursued a career in literature, writing several books before he passed in 1916. Francis penned the books - "Ballads and Poems from the Pacific," "Under Western Skies" and "From the Four Winds."

After Isabella passed away, Francis Sinclair Jr. married his deceased wife's widowed sister, who was also his cousin.

Neither marriage resulted in children and after selling all his interest in Ni'ihau, the original brothers listed on the deed of sale for Ni'ihau were no longer associated with the island. Their time had come and gone in the first two generations of the family in their new home they had made for themselves. They were passing the torch to the next generation to steward the island of Ni'ihau, which at that time had not yet earned the nickname "The Forbidden Island". That name came even after the Ni'ihau incident with Shigenori Nishikaichi but would start with Audrey Robinson.

As the 1800s came to a close, the island of Ni'ihau was now managed by Audrey Robinson, who took over in part when Francis Jr. gave his two nephews (Audrey and Francis Gay) control of the island. Audrey and Francis Gay were cousins and also brothers-in-law.

In Makaweli, the two cousins formed the Gay & Robinson Company in 1889, which still operates on Kaua'i and Ni'ihau to this day. As sugar production ramped up on Kaua'i in the early 20th century, the Gay & Robinson Company kept up with the progress and shifted their ranch towards sugarcane production, which would be the main stream of revenue for the family over the course of the next 100 years.

Audrey Robinson was well educated, having been taught at home in his early life. He attended college at the Boston University School of Law. Audrey was admitted to the bar in eastern courts and traveled Europe and Asia before returning home to Makaweli to manage Ni'ihau and the ranch on Kaua'i.

Audrey was born in New Zealand on October 17, 1853. He was 10 years old when his grandmother Elizabeth purchased the island in the name of his uncles James and Francis. His mother was Helen Sinclair, the daughter of Elizabeth. His mother married Charles Barrington Robinson, an Englander who had made some acclaim in New Zealand where he met Audrey's mother Helen, marrying her in 1843. Audrey came as their gift of toil and prosperity in New Zealand with the family eventually selling their New Zealand holdings prior to relocating to Hawaii. Charles Robinson and Helen moved to England in 1863 after selling their New Zealand property and remained there until Charles died in 1899 in Richmond, Surrey.

After his father's passing in 1899, and then his grandmother's a year later in 1900, Audrey came into his own as the manager of the family's land in Hawai'i. Employing new strategies like when the family imported Arabian horses for breeding purposes in 1884 under the supervision of Audrey. In the early years of Audrey's management, the family imported Merino sheep, shorthorn cattle, as well as other purebred sheep and cattle. The Gay & Robinson company used the island of Ni'ihau exclusively for grazing their livestock, in addition to their land in Makaweli, Kauai. By the turn of the century, as the shift towards more sugar cane production necessitated more land use, the family leased 6,000 acres of their Makaweli estate on Kauai to the Hawaiian Sugar Company.

In 1888, Audrey and Alice Gay Robinson welcomed Alymer into the world. His brother Lester followed in 1901, giving the Robinsons the eventual heirs that would continue the legacy well into the future.

Audrey stepped down as the manager of the family's ranch operation in Ni'ihau and Kaua'i in 1912, passing the title of foreman to his sons Alymer and Lester, who were separated in age by 13 years. Alymer was the eldest of the two, and the pair would deliver the island of Ni'ihau into the era that would usher in the name "The Forbidden Island" to Ni'ihau.

Audrey Robinson passed away in 1936 at 82 years old, leaving his two sons with the responsibility that comes with being the owners of Niihau. Sugarcane reached its peak in the 1930s in Hawaii with more than 30% of all jobs coming from the production of sugar, or distribution. Prior to his passing, Audrey Robinson was credited with restricting visitors to the island first in 1915. Visitation was restricted on a permission-only basis from the Robinsons. The practice never stopped from 1915 on and is still the common practice in the modern day.

Alymer managed Ni'ihau, while his younger brother Lester took care of the Kaua'i operations. Alymer transitioned Ni'ihau from the time of Audrey to the times of the Ni'ihau incident and another world war.

President Franklin D. Roosevelt visited Hawai'i in 1934 and suggested Ni'ihau as a loaction for the United Nations headquarters in 1944. Serious consideration was given to this by the government, but never materialized.

After the Ni'ihau incident brought more attention to the island than there had ever been before post Ni'ihau Incident, a terrible threat starting in the 1950s came in the form of a polio plague that swept across the archipelago, peaking in 1952.

The Robinsons and Ni'ihau had by then become one, as the island and the people have intertwined since they had come to steward the land as the rightful owners. In order to protect the family from the plague that threatened the entire island's population, and visitors that had brought sickness and trouble, the family decided to close off the island to all visitors.

Although the island has a restrictive nature

intrinsically, and geographically, visitors would still make their way to the island for myriads of reasons. In 1952, with a susceptible population, the choice was made to completely halt all visitation. In a nod to the future, the Robinson family made anyone returning to the island quarantine for two weeks. Still coming to terms with the aftermath of the Ni'ihau Incident, the Robinson family put extreme measures in place 11 years after Shigenori made his unwelcome entrance onto the island. There was a reluctance to accept anyone who came to the island after the Ni'ihau incident, and the polio plague further enhanced these fears on Ni'ihau.

Sitting in the middle of the ocean, with the Pacific Ocean as an idyllic blanket wrapping the island in safety, the Robinson family was free to make their lives as they saw fit. They were unburdened by what was happening in the mainland and in the rest of the state, content with working the land the way it had been in the days of the Hawaiian Kingdom.

And the family felt as if they were honoring their word to the king in this way. They felt that it was truly in the interest of the Hawaiian people and the residents to live in this manner. They were not charged for living there, but would rather work for their lodging.

And the island remained fixed, as it had for millions of years beforehand like it was waiting all the while for someone to call it home.

And as time went on, the measures put in

place to protect against a plague of polio besieg-
ing the Hawaiian islands in 1952 remained in ef-
fect after fear of polio had long faded away. The
Robinson family made the decision, like many
they had in the past, precise and for a reason. The
reason suited the inhabitants of the island, essen-
tially drawing a line in the sand between the rest
of Hawai'i and Ni'ihau. There was the rest of the
world, as far as they were concerned, and then
there was the island. This is how it had been in
the past, and this is how they felt it needed to be
going into the future.

This is what earned the pristine island the
name that it has earned over the centuries as the
forbidden island.

It remained forbidden until a deal was made
with the new owners of the island, who took over
after Alymer and Lester guided the Robinson family through another generation of ownership,
handing it down to the next.

The brothers passed away within two years
of each other, despite the vast difference of thir-
teen years of age between the two. Alymer died
in 1967 at 78 years old when the country was in
change like no other it had seen in the past. Lester
joined Alymer in death two years later, passing
away in 1969. Neither brother made it out of the
1960's but left behind a keen sense of the past in
the way they had done things.

And with the gift of stewardship, the new
owners had vision for the future. These new vi-
sions found their hardships at the end of the 20th

century as the Robinson family was now guided by the dutiful hands of Lester's two sons - Keith and Bruce Robinson. The two brothers gained ownership of the island and the Kaua'i holdings in 2002 when Lester's wife Helen (Matthew Robinson) passed away in 2002.

In the time after the passing of Alymer and Lester in the 1970s, Hawai'i governor John Burns made multiple an attempts to purchase Ni'ihau for $300,000 through the legislature. It was an offer that Bruce, Keith, and Helen denied.

Keith was quoted at the time as saying, "We could be offered all the gold in the world and it wouldn't make any difference. Some things are more important than money."

The brothers had really taken over when Alymer began to pass the torch, and then when he passed away. The boys were in their 20s when Alymer and Lester passed away, and the world was in the flux of the 1960s and 1970s. Hawai'i had seen Elvis come and go on Kaua'i by the time Lester passed away.

For the next 50 plus years, the two brothers have managed the island and the property on Kaua'i with the same reverence for the land, and the same work ethic that defined earlier managers. The Gay & Robinson company set a world record for sugarcane production in 1987, producing 17.42 tons of sugar per acre. This mark was the peak production point for the company, and during the 1990s, the state saw a sharp decline in sugarcane production and revenue. Sugarcane had reached the peak production point it would ever gain on Kaua'i via the Robinsons by then. As the sugarcane industry declined in the 90s, the ranch on Niihau faced economic challenges.

The brothers continued the legacy of their ancestors who had come before them. They did not charge any of the residents to reside on the island and Keith is credited with keeping several species of plants from going extinct.

Keith was born the year Shigenori landed on the island of Ni'ihau in 1941. He has continued the stewardship of the island and started his journey by attending the University of California, Davis as a youth. He later graduated with a degree in agronomy and ranch management before enlisting in the Army. After serving, he went to work at the Ko'olau Ranch ranch in Oahu for several years. After working at the ranch in Oahu and serving in the Army, Keith Robinson turned to commercial fishing. Robinson operated a commercial fishing venture for seven years before he took to the family business with his brother Bruce for the rest of his life, devoting every part of his existence to the two islands.

On July 26, 1997, Keith Robinson wrote an opinion editorial to the Honolulu Star-Bulletin titled "Our private paradise".

"Niihau isn't the backward little stone-age concentration camp that most of the outside world probably thinks it is, but it is private. We bought Niihau fairly, squarely and honestly, and the island is our private property.

"The Niihau people who live there are, legally, our guests. Unlike tenants, they pay no rent and there are no formal contractual obligations.

"For private reasons of our own, we have for decades given those guests free but revocable privileges that are probably far greater than those allowed by any other landowner in America.

"They are given free housing. They also have unlimited supplies of free mutton and pork, and beef is available to them at prices far below what the general public pays.

"They also get free transportation on Niihau Ranch trucks and free transportation of their supplies and belongings on the Niihau Ranch barge.

"For almost a century, we have reserved some 200 acres of good land for their vegetable gardens, immediately adjacent to Puuwai village. Anyone who wants to grow vegetables there has only to ask; but for about 30 years, no one has gardened there.

"They have free hunting, fishing, camping and sightseeing access to every part of a relatively unspoiled private island -- probably the only place in all Hawaii and maybe even the entire United States where this occurs. We have carefully maintained the privacy of their community, and also have not permitted the kind of immigration and settlement that has submerged and destroyed the Hawaiian language and culture everywhere else in Hawaii.

"From time to time, we also have established programs and policies designed to protect the health and welfare of those guests. As a direct result of this, Niihau was probably the only island in all Hawaii to escape the great polio epidemic that swept the U.S. in the 1950s.

"It was also the only Hawaiian island to be totally vaccinated (for free) during the so-called "swine flu" scare some 10-15 years ago.

"I suspect that, at present, it is the only Hawaiian island that has never had a case of AIDS. Our drug problem is also far smaller than those of other communities in Hawaii.

"When it comes to business matters, the job opportunities on Niihau are reserved for these same guests. We preferentially hire from among them. We employ about 2-3 times as many people as we actually need.

"I estimate that we have lost somewhere between $8-9 million trying to keep people employed. This figure does not count income loss from giving free housing and free meat to a community of 150-200 people.

"On top of everything else, we give these same guests a certain amount of advisory input into our affairs, and often try to accommodate their wishes.

"For example, their village and favorite shell-gathering beaches have been reserved for them by wide exclusion zones in our military project planning.

"To put it bluntly, I don't know of any other landowner anywhere in the United States who does nearly as much for guests as we do. During the past century, they have received an enormous amount of privileges and benefits from us.

"Now, in exchange for those privileges and benefits, we do require certain things.

"First and foremost, we require that they shall not do or say anything that adversely affects our constitutional right to enjoy the security and privacy of our property and business affairs.

"We have been severely hammered in the past by Hawaii's ruling political machine. That situation eventually became so flagrant that, at one point, one of their bureaucrats openly and casually admitted they were deliberately discriminating against us. We now intensely distrust the political machine, and feel that the less known about our affairs, the less damage will be done to us.

"In addition, the Niihau people clearly understand that the less the outside world knows about our property, the less trouble we and they will have with theft, vandalism, trespassing and destructive meddling.

"Above all else, discussion with outsiders of national defense research projects being conducted on the island is taboo. The national security is to be strictly respected and upheld.

"There have been times when this silence was critical. For example, part of the research that established the Distant Early Warning Line -- the great shield that first protected Americans and the free world from surprise missile attack --

was done in intense secrecy on Niihau.

"Nobody there talked, the project was successfully completed and Russia was prevented from being able to cripple the U.S. with a nuclear "Pearl Harbor."

"We still require that same silence today, both to maintain our constitutional right to security and privacy, and to protect the security of any national defense projects we may undertake.

"The second thing that we require of Niihau residents is that they maintain a reasonably honest, sober and moral lifestyle as long as they are living on our property. Anybody who does not do so is subject to possible expulsion.

"The Robinson family operations include a one-of-a-kind upland endangered species reserve and marine endangered species preservation. Among other things, Niihau is apparently the only island in the world that has been successfully recolonized by monk seals in the present century.

"I wouldn't go so far as to say that we have created a conservation empire. But the hard fact remains that a lot of things that have disappeared everywhere else still survive on our land, like endangered species, clean streams, Hawaiian-speaking communities, etc.

"For more than half a century, we have managed to successfully balance all of these different and sometimes conflicting parts of our operation, including agricultural business, national defense research, environmental conservation and cultural preservation.

"This work hasn't been cheap or easy, and most of the time we were being badly strained, both physically and financially. Since we are human, we have made our share of mistakes along the way.

"We often have been the target of all sorts of criticism from politicians and activists and the news media.

"This situation will no doubt regularly continue. But now we are used to it. Political mud-slingers, screaming activists and cesspool-diving journalists are a basic part of modern life.

"But when everything else is said and done, one hard fact remains: For more than half a century, we have consistently accomplished all sorts of things, especially preservation and conservation work that none of our critics ever did. And we continue to stand squarely on our constitutional rights to do our work, especially national defense work, in the security and privacy of our own property.

"In the long run, no situation has ever remained unchanged throughout human history. We will try to maintain the place as long as we reasonably can, but can obviously make no permanent guarantees.

"Several years ago, after many decades of relative prosperity in the sugar business, Hawaii's economy finally began to wither under heavy government regulation and taxation.

"Today the state's agricultural self-sufficiency has been completely destroyed, and hard times exist everywhere. At the moment, we have very little extra money to subsidize Niihau.

"Under these circumstances, it is rather incredible that a single family has somehow managed to maintain an entire community for so long."

Keith's opinion editorial to the Star-Bulletin marked the beginning of a new era for the island and the family. It was a new era of media attention for different reasons than the Ni'ihau Incident, or the Robinson family. It was the attention that now focused on the island itself and what the preservation of the island means to Hawai'i and the Hawaiian culture that had been in some form preserved on Ni'ihau.

In 1999, after operating for 135 years, the ranch on Ni'ihau was officially closed down. When the ranch was closed, the only employer on the island was lost to the 120 residents at the time.

Keith would go on to declare after the ranch closed in 1999, "Cattle ranching is dead. Sheep ranching is dead. Honey is dead. Even charcoal is dead."

The brothers decided the island of Nii'hau at the turn of the century would again be opened up for visits from foreigners. A deal allowed visitors to come to the island for $630 a person. There was a hunting safari offered for visitors to come and hunt some of the island's big game, like goats and pigs. There was also an excursion that dropped visitors off via a helicopter on the north shore of Ni'ihau at Nanina Beach. Visitors were allowed to explore the island for only three and a half hours before having to depart. Interaction with the villagers was kept at a minimum and the island was once again a destination to explore the hidden wonders that had remained of limits for 85 years.

When another pandemic threatened the residents of Ni'ihau in March of 2020, the Robinson family again made the decision to halt visitation to the island. Any family or essential visitors were again required to quarantine for two weeks before interacting with the residents.

The tours resumed after the COVID-19 pandemic, with the family opting to keep visits operating on a limited basis. In 2022, the Robinsons were granted an annual flat rate tax of $40,000 by the county of Kaua'i in light of the family's contribution to the Hawaiian people and the residents who have lived on the island with their cultural integrity still intact.

The move by the county of Kaua'i to impose a flat rate tax rate on the island came at a time when billionaires were once again buying up huge swaths of land in the islands.

Mark Zuckerberg had acquired 700 acres of land on Kaua'i just three years prior to the county of Kaua'i imposing a flat rate tax fee on the Robinson family that can be changed at "anytime". The rate is well below the $130,000 the family was assessed in property taxes in 2022 and 2023. The flat rate property tax of $40,000 can be changed at any time by the Kaua'i County Council as Ni'ihau is part of the county of Kaua'i, even though it receives no road maintenance, rubbish collection, police, or fire protection.

"There are so many billionaires that are here in Hawai'i that want a piece of this heaven," Kaua'i County Councilman Billy DeCosta said of the flat rate fee in 2022. "Ni'ihau is one area that we felt as politicians we could assist the landowners with the tax revenue that they would have to pay based on what they do for the community, the Native Hawaiian people of Ni'ihau and what services we as a county don't provide."

With the ranch no longer operating and the two brothers who now own the island in their 80's, the future of the island is uncertain. It has always been a paradise hidden from the rest of the world, but as the world has changed over the years the island has managed to stay similar to the day the Robinson family stepped foot on the forbidden island.

The island has changed too. The animals that call the island home were mostly brought there over the decades, and that has shaped the flora on the island tremendously. The plants that were brought there changed the island, and it is always changing with the people that inhabit the island. The number of people living on the island was recorded as 80 in the 2020 census. They live in the traditional way, with bike and horse being their main mode of transportation. On nearby Kauai, the people live with the modern comfort of technology and many of the residents of Ni'ihau frequent Kaua'i, but Ni'ihau remains steadfast as a reminder of the old way of Hawaii. A way that has changed on all the other islands, but remains on Ni'ihau.

In 2010 Keith Robinson wrote a book titled "Approach to Armageddon, One Christian's Speculation About the End of the Age." The 476-page book was published by Destiny Publishers out of Merrimac, Massachusetts

Keith's description of the book read, "Approach to Armageddon, which took more than ten years to research and write, can best be described as a defense of the King James Bible and the Protestant Christian faith generally. It points out that (a) the ancient Bible prophecies appear to be far more relevant and accurate than anything in East-ern Mysticism, the Mayan Calendar, Nostradamus, or the Da Vinci Code, and (b) that the United States and Great Britain have made disastrous national mistakes, which may ultimately lead to the rise of the Anti-Christ, and to a worldwide nuclear war."

Now at 84 years old, Keith Robinson and his brother are the last of another generation that has brought the island through the generations of family ownership. With the impending transition, the next generation of the Robinson family will have to navigate another era of change as the island of Ni'ihau remains fixed in the Pacific Ocean, safely tucked away as a jewel of the Hawaiian Archipelago. It sits, waiting in the wings, forbidden to any visitors who want to come without invitation.

In 2024 there were 22 votes cast in the presedential election on the island. Of those votes, 21 were for the republican nominee Donald Trump. Only one of the 23 votes was democratic, making Ni'ihau the only district in Hawai'i that voted over 90% republican. In 2020, 100% of the Ni'ihau vote, or 43 votes went for the republican nominee Donald Trump. Zero votes were cast for the democratic nominee Joe Biden.

The forbidden island will continue to fascinate the imagination of those who cannot go to the island and it remains as the final bastion of the Hawaiian Kingdom. It will remain that way until the waves of the outside world make their descent once again onto the sands of Ni'ihau as they did on December 1, 1941. The only thing that is certain is that people will keep coming, and change will always be with them.

The only piece of the island available to those who want to acquire it comes in the form of the Ni'ihau shell lei. The lei is crafted from the Ni'ihau shells that only come from the forbidden island. The tiny shells are carefully collected and are stranded together in elaborate designs that feature strands and vibrant colors. The necklaces were worn by Hawaiian royalty in the days of the Hawaiian Kingdom and the necklaces have made their way back to the limelight as a visual representation of the forbidden island and a reminder of the treasure that comes from the place and the people that reside there. A single necklace can sell for thousands of dollars and a bill signed by Hawai'i governor Linda Lingle in 2004 protects Ni'ihau shell leis from conterfeiting.

The island of Ni'ihau is the forbidden island, a name that has been earned through generations of toil and hard work, standing back firmly against the rest of the world. It has remained forbidden from celebrities, government, and those who wish to take it from the family who made it their home so long ago. And it will remain this way, even as the sun sets behind the island on a winter day in Kaua'i, turning the forbidden island into a hue of gold that cannot be described in words, but can only be experienced as the sun fades away with a ceremonial flash of green.

"Kaua'i steals the sun, Ni'ihau is the sun. Kaua'i is where the sun rises, but Ni'ihau is where it sets."

Ben Kanehale (left) receiving decorations in August 1945

Officials point out the crash site in 1941

A Niihau village as seen in 1885

Keith Robinson drinks from a stream in Makaweli

Shigenori Ishikaitchi's crashed zero on December 17, 1941

'Indigenous Flowers of the Hawaiian Islands'
published 1885 by Isabella Sinclair

Rare photograph. Aylmer Robinson, left, his brother Lester, and Governor Quinn right, Niihau, 1961

Howard Kaleohano

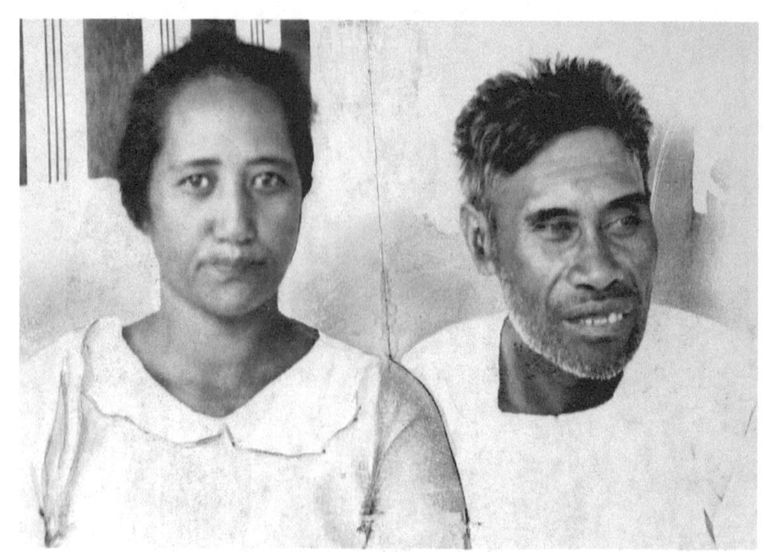

Ben and Ella Kanehale

Rusted wreckage of Shigenori's zero at the Pacific
Aviation Museum in Pearl Harbor

Ishikaichi Shigenori

A 20 caliber machine gun from Nishikaichi's plane

Niihau shell leis in a koa box

An illustration of "Atooi" (Waimea) in 1778

Elizabeth Sinclair circa 1885

King Kamehameha V circa 1864

JOHN EDGAR HOOVER
DIRECTOR

2-0

Federal Bureau of Investigation
United States Department of Justice
Washington, D. C.

MAR 20 1942

PERSONAL AND ~~CONFIDENTIAL~~
BY SPECIAL MESSENGER

Major General Edwin M. Watson
Secretary to the President
The White House
Washington, D. C.

Dear General Watson:

I thought the President and you might be interested in the incident of a Japanese pilot being forced down in his plane on December 7, 1941, on the outlying Island of Niihau, Territory of Hawaii, where, with the aid of two Japanese, one a citizen and one an alien, he gained possession of firearms and terrorized the natives, who were ignorant of the existence of war, until overcome and killed on December 13, 1941, by a Hawaiian native he had shot and wounded. A memorandum covering the details of this incident is transmitted herewith.

With assurances of my highest regards,

Sincerely,

J. E. Hoover

Enclosure

M E M O R A N D U M

On Sunday, December 7, 1941, between 1:00 p.m. and 2:00 p.m., the natives of the outlying Island of Niihau, Territory of Hawaii, observed two airplanes flying low over the island. One flew on west past the island and was not seen again. The other, apparently out of gasoline, crashed near the home of Howard Kaleohano, a native Hawaiian on the outskirts of Nonopapa Village. Kaleohano rushed to the plane, which to his surprise he noted was not American, and, observing the Japanese pilot therein, pistol in hand, trying to disengage himself from his safety belt, wrenched the pistol from him and pulled the pilot out of the plane. Kaleohano also searched the pilot and his plane, securing all papers, which included a map of Oahu, the main Hawaiian Island on which the city of Honolulu, the Pearl Harbor Naval Base, and other important military installations are located.

By that time the native Hawaiian population from Nonopapa Village arrived on the scene and the pilot surrendered. The pilot, whose name was never ascertained, appeared friendly and peaceful and therefore at first was not held in custody, but was allowed to roam free, being fed and sheltered in the home of one of the natives. At first, when spoken to, he would reply in English writing, but later he spoke fluent English to the native populace. Possibly he was educated on the American Mainland.

It should be noted that the residents of the Island of Niihau, at that time, did not know of the existence of a state of war between the United States and Japan, nor of the Japanese raids on the Pearl Harbor Naval Base. The Island of Niihau has no communication with the other islands of the Hawaiian group, except by boat, and no boat stopped at that island from the outbreak of hostilities until Sunday morning, December 14, 1941. During the intervening period, however, on Monday and Tuesday, December 8 and 9, 1941, the natives took the aviator to Keei, where a sampan from the Island of Kauai was expected to call, in order to send him back to the proper authorities. The sampan didn't show up, and they could not launch a whaleboat stationed there because the sea was too rough. Also, on the night of Friday, December 12, 1941, the natives attempted, from the top of Paniau, the highest mountain on Niihau, to signal the Island of Kauai, by means of kerosene lamps and reflectors, but it does not appear that these messages got through to Kauai.

On Wednesday, December 10, 1941, the pilot was placed under loose guard at the home of Yoshio Harada, a Japanese of American citizenship. On Thursday, Harada sent a message to Ishimatsu Shintani, a Japanese alien resident on Niihau, to come to see him. These were the only two Japanese on the island. On Friday morning, December 12, 1941, Shintani went to Harada's house and there conferred with the Japanese pilot and Harada. The Hawaiians on guard at the Harada house do not know what they talked about, as they conversed in the Japanese language.

On Friday, December 12, 1941, Shintani went to the house of Kaleohano and attempted to obtain from him the papers Kaleohano had taken from the pilot and out of his plane. Shintani stated it was a "life and death matter", and indicated he desired to destroy the papers by burning. Kaleohano showed the papers to Shintani, but refused to give them to him, even though Shintani offered a money bribe of about $200.00.

Sometime during Friday afternoon, the Japanese pilot, under guard at Harada's house, by Harada and a Hawaiian native, cooperated with Harada to overpower the Hawaiian guard and secure Harada's shotgun. The aviator and Harada locked the guard in one of Harada's warehouses. They then stopped a native Hawaiian woman on the nearby road, ordered her and her children, at the point of the shotgun, to dismount from her horse-drawn wagon, commandeered it, and drove off in the direction of the plane crash.

At the scene of the plane crash, they found a sixteen year old boy guarding the plane. Kaleohano observed the aviator, Harada, and the boy approaching his house at about 5:30 p.m., Harada prodding the boy in the back with his shotgun. Kaleohano hid from them in his outhouse. They entered Kaleohano's home, searched it, and apparently recovered the Japanese pilot's pistol which Kaleohano had taken from him at the time of the crash. When they left and went back to the plane, Kaleohano came out of hiding and changed the papers to another hiding place away from his house. Kaleohano then gave the alarm to Nonopapa Village that the men were on the rampage and most of the native populace fled to the mountains or the forest.

About dusk Friday, the aviator and Harada captured two native Hawaiians and forced them to help dismount the two machine guns from the plane, loading them and a large pile of cartridges onto the wagon which they had commandeered. The captives heard and observed the Japanese pilot get into the plane, turn on the radio, put on the earphones, and make calls, talking in Japanese. However, they did not hear him receive any reply.

One of these Hawaiians escaped from the aviator and Harada, and went to the beach where he enlisted the aid of Benny Nokaka Kanahele in attempting to secure the cartridges which had been removed from the plane, inasmuch as Harada had told him that there were enough cartridges there to kill every man, woman, and child on the island. He and Kanahele went to the wagon and found it deserted and unguarded. Harada and the aviator had gone off seeking to find more natives, and apparently took the machine guns with them, as they were not on the wagon. Kanahele and the other Hawaiian took the cartridges and hid them on the beach.

During Friday night and early Saturday morning, the aviator and Harada burned the plane and Kaleohano's house, evidently hoping to destroy the aviator's papers in the conflagration. They also went through Nonopapa Village shooting off their guns and otherwise terrorizing the natives, most of whom had fled into the forest and to the mountains. No natives were killed, but they captured several, including Benny Kanahele and his wife.

On Saturday, December 13, 1941, at about 10:00 a.m., Kanahele attempted to snatch the pistol from his captor, the pilot, but failed. Kanahele's wife, who was next to him, then grabbed for the pistol and Harada snatched her away. The pilot, who still retained his pistol, shot Kanahele three times, inflicting flesh wounds in the right and left thighs and on his upper right side. Kanahele then picked up the pilot bodily and dashed his head against a stone wall killing him. Harada thereupon turned his gun on himself, shot himself twice in the abdomen, and died soon afterward.

Early Saturday morning, December 13, 1941, at 12:30 a.m., six strong Hawaiians, including Kaleohano, launched the whaleboat at Keei and after a trip of about 15 hours, rowed to the Island of Kauai, Territory of Hawaii, where they reported to Elmer Robinson, an American resident, who reported to the American Naval authorities, the facts as to the presence of the Japanese pilot on the Island of Niihau, and how, with the aid of the two Japanese on the island, they had terrorized and intimidated the native populace. A squad of twelve soldiers left Kauai late Saturday afternoon, aboard a lighthouse tender, arriving at the Island of Niihau on Sunday morning, December 14, 1941, where they found that the pilot and Harada had already been disposed of. Shintani, the alien Japanese who had tried to bribe Kaleohano and Mrs. Ymeno Harada, the wife of the Japanese citizen, were arrested and are now incarcerated at Wailua Jail, on the Island of Kauai, in the custody of the military authorities. Benny Kanahele and his wife were also brought back to Kauai and given medical treatment.

9 781956 881578